I looked at Tom.

He had his arms up [illegible]
blood, not water, was dripping from them.

I looked at Ann.

She had no shoes. Her right foot was bare; a couple of flies dropped down onto it. The other foot wore a green sock with a letter *S* in white. Her legs were fat and sleek, as though they had somehow been inflated. So, too, was the rest of her.

Her eyes were deeply sunk in her puffy face. But for the strawberry birthmark stark on her neck and bared now to the world, I wouldn't have known her.

Flies were zipping in by dozens and I saw yellow jackets among them. There'd soon be more. Three settled around her eyes; I brushed them off. The sight of them made me frantic. I scrambled to my feet.

★

Hewitt Schlereth

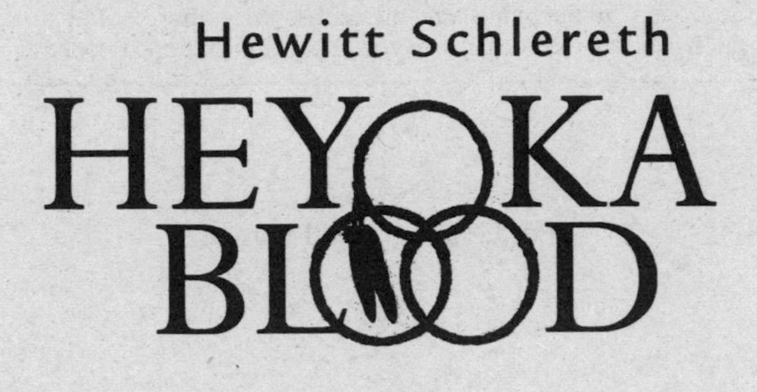

TORONTO • NEW YORK • LONDON
AMSTERDAM • PARIS • SYDNEY • HAMBURG
STOCKHOLM • ATHENS • TOKYO • MILAN
MADRID • WARSAW • BUDAPEST • AUCKLAND

For Grace, so well named.

HEYOKA BLOOD

A Worldwide Mystery/February 2006

First published by Hilliard & Harris.

ISBN 0-373-26556-5

Printed in U.S.A.

Acknowledgments

In 1955 or thereabouts, I read *The Natural Superiority of Women* by Ashley Montagu, and looking at the main women in my life at the time—my grandmother, my mother, my sister—I could see the guy was onto something. Whether I can fairly lay the blame for my fictional matriarchal nation of Heyoka on Ashley Montagu is moot; so let's just say his work was an eye-opener and a watershed, but I am the main culprit. There were, of course, abettors aplenty—family, friends, unlucky dinner partners; in short, too many to name. I must, however, say particular thanks to two who kept me writing till the book was done: Louise Ladd of Fairfield University's Writing for Publication workshop, and Trudy Seagraves of the Nutmeg Writer's Group.

HEYOKA:

Small, oil-producing American Indian nation in coastal New England. Governance is traditionally entirely female (See also: Matriarchies, Contemporary). It consists of a mainland portion and three islands: Arkady, Eskar and Flyaway. The word *Heyoka* is said to mean The Strong Women.

—*The Dictionary of Little-Known American Places*

ONE

THERE ARE WATERY GRAVES; there are watery lives. My own aquatic being begins at the end of dock A in the Arkady Island Marina. I live there on my boat.

I had been up all night reading a pre-publication copy of my book. I was eye-sore and weary; felt I'd earned my coming gratifications—vodka on ice, my capacious bunk, eine kleine Mozart twinkling from the stereo.

My hand was in the fridge for the ice when my boat swayed and her mooring lines creaked as someone came aboard.

I waited. Not a sound, but the boat continued to rock. Someone big, careful with his step. The doorway darkened.

"It's me, Hadrian. Tom."

I relaxed and pulled out a tray of ice. "Thomas, it's seven bells in the graveyard watch; almost dawn. I see Venus through the porthole down here. We should be asleep." I twisted the tray over a tumbler and most of the cubes showered into it; the rest clattered into the sink, sounding very loud.

"Hadrian, there's something spooky out here."

"What sort of something?" Tom has sharp eyes and he does not spook easily. Whatever it was, I'd have to look. With an inward sigh, I set the ice tray in the sink.

Tom said, "I think it's a body."

My heart skidded. I knew he thought it was Ann Summerlune who hadn't been seen in three weeks. Ogod, please no, my old flame is too young to die.

I pushed the refrigerator door slowly to, and climbed the stairs to the pilot house. Tom is an inch over my six-two, but much wider. He filled the doorway, strangling a pair of binoculars in one huge hand, but otherwise not showing his tension. I pulled my binoculars from their bin by the chart table and followed him toward the bow.

All was gray; the water mirror-calm, reflecting no stars, only bright Venus; the other boats around us in a silent wall; our shoes squeaking in the dew on the deck.

Tom pointed over the bow rail, whispered, "There, Hade, in the middle of the basin, about a hundred feet from the fuel dock." He raised his binoculars and I saw what he meant—a blob, a tiny atoll in the slick water. I swung my binoculars to my eyes and focused. Magnified seven times, it was still a blob. Might be a lot of things, I thought.

"Tom, it's a dead skunk, or a tire, or a waterlogged stump. We've had a lot of rain lately; it's just some of the junk that always gets washed down the rivers and into the harbors." I lowered the binocs and inspected Tom.

Maybe my old shipmate had been living a bit too high at the Three O's Salooon? No, not Tom.

"Tom, we're both up too early and out too late. You see a corpse, I see a cat. Remember the Memorial Day we were riding the Stream off Hatteras and it started to snow? By the end of the watch, we were so cold and drained you were seeing rocks and to me the waves were crocodiles?"

Tom eyed me. We've been friends for damn near forty years. I could feel his temperature rising. With one hand he gripped the back of my head and forced my gaze to the lump in the water.

"Look, Wallace. Watch close. Every now and then the water heaves. Wait..." The water swayed. Tom shook my head. "See?" Another sway, another shake. "Look at the surface to the left of the lump." I saw. A slight bulge, as though the water were about to blister. Like a flat sea the instant before a whale breaks through. My stomach joined the slide of my heart. I lifted my glasses again.

But the sun had broken the night; the sky was scarlet; the water wore blood. Now I could see nothing. And there was a tremor in my hands. I took a breath, wound the strap around the glasses and said, "I guess we'd better get the dinghy and have a look."

"Shouldn't we call the police first?"

In retrospect, we should have, but despite the unease of my heart and the rising skirl in my gut, I clung to the hope of flotsam after a rain.

"Tom, if it turns out to be a dead raccoon or a chunk of junk, we'll look like sixteen kinds of idiot. If it is a body we'll call then."

"Okay," he said. Then, seeing my skiff lashed into its cradle on the cabin top, "We'll take my dink. It's in."

Lights were coming on in the boats around us and at the fuel dock. I leaned into the pilot house, dropped the binoculars into their holder, snatched my cell phone, and we ran as quick as we could over the damp planking of the floats.

Tom's fat old steel ketch barely moved as we leapt aboard. His dinghy was tied off at the end of the mizzen boom to keep it from thumping the hull. Tom untied and tugged and when the dinghy touched the stern, let the thin rope fall onto the heavier one coiled on top of the dink's anchor. He dropped down, straddling the center seat, and held on while I lowered myself into the stern. With the two of us, the water was close to the top edge of the little boat. Tom rowed carefully, the oarlocks clicking softly.

As we drew near, he turned the boat and backed toward the black whatever-it-was.

It was a human head, and it was abuzz with flies. The fan of dark hair around it swayed in the light swell. Ann's hair was dark, and she always wore it long to mask a strawberry mark on her neck. "Closer," I whispered through a tight throat.

Tom edged us in. Below the surface I now saw a

white shirt with a collar. To cover her birthmark Ann usually wore shirts with collars.

My throat was so tight now I wasn't sure I could talk. I pushed out a wispy "Pass me an oar."

The brass oarlock rattled as Tom lifted an oar and slid it into my back-stretched hand. With it, I pushed at the mass of undulant hair.

My hands were so cold the water felt warm. I picked up an odor a lot like skunk, but clenched my teeth and forced the oar farther. An ear came clear. With the tip of the blade, I levered the collar down and there was her birthmark, raw as a wound, red as the dawn.

"It's Ann." I dropped the oar.

Flies exploded into the air and whined onto us. Flailing at them with one hand I got the oar, tossed it to Tom and opened my cell phone while Tom used the oar to paddle us clear.

The boat turned from the lopsided thrust, and I was caught full in the face by the sun. I winced away and my dazzled eyes picked up a fishing boat running toward us, its lights still on, its nets swaying in swags. From its bow wave, hundreds of sparks were shooting into the air; falling; flashing up again. Minnows and menhaden leaping for their lives before a pack of bluefish!

My heart and my stomach congealed. That gang of saltwater piranha was going to slam right into Ann.

Tom saw me staring and looked over his shoulder.

"What the..?" His glance froze on the boil of baitfish. "Oshit. Blues."

"Tom," I wheezed, "we have to tow Ann ashore…get her out of the water…" I pointed. "Fuel dock."

He snatched up the other oar, slammed it into its lock. The little boat's joints creaked and cracked as he forced us toward Ann again. Retching, I pushed an arm into the stinging flies to grab her hair.

Oshit, I was still holding the cell phone.

I let it fall into the water and scooped up a mushy handful of hair. Turning to sit, I came off my knees, lost my balance. My butt landed on the transom. The back of the boat went under. Water poured in.

Instinctively, Tom strained away from me to get the stern up. "Hadrian! For crying out loud! We don't want to be in the water with a pack of blues! Leave her. We'll call 911 from shore." His voice wavered as I had never heard it before. Tom, my rock in many a jam, wobbly as I was.

I too lurched toward the bow to level the boat, and Ann's hair came out in my hand. I threw the sodden mess from me and hissed at Tom, "Dammit, man, I will not leave her to the blues."

Tom's eyes slitted, his big flat face went paler than I'd ever seen it. I was asking too much.

I lunged past him, grabbed the end of the anchor

line, yanked off my shoes, whacked Tom's shoulder and croaked, "I'll get a loop around her. Take the rope to the dock and pull her in. I'll swim."

He blinked. I shook his arm, put my face right up to his, "Tom, just—do—it."

Tom said nothing. For an instant I thought he would swat me overboard. But without a word, he stretched out to take a full sweep with the oars and I slid hastily in. The water was thin, didn't want to hold me up, wanted me under. I could feel those torpedoes with teeth hurtling at me. Why wasn't Tom moving? I slapped the transom of the dink. "Tom!" He was frozen. I coiled up and shoved the dink with my feet, "Tom! Go! Go!"

Down slashed the oars. The water leapt into foam. With a crack, the little boat shot away. I prayed to the rope flowing over the transom: Ogod, don't snag, don't snag, and turned to save Ann.

By the time Tom reached the dock, I had a bowline around her and was yelling for him to haul. Trailing the line, he leaped from the dinghy, turned and hauled so fast his hands were a blur. The rope came taut with a twang and a bloom of spray. Ann's body surged away.

As I rolled into the fastest Australian crawl I ever did, my eyes took in the oncoming fishing boat and the geyser of baitfish dancing above the razor jaws beneath.

Fishboat, baitfish, bluefish, me-charging for the fuel dock.

TWO

THE BAITFISH AND I barely beat the blues. Sensing the dock, most of the little guys veered away, but many overshot and I flopped onto the dock under a shower of sardines.

About as frantic now as the hunted fish, I scrambled to my knees. Tom held Ann by the rope, the whites of his eyes startling as he stared at me. I grabbed Ann's arm and wobbled to my feet.

All around, I heard a rapid-fire slamming of locker lids as fishermen dove for their poles.

Ann's arm felt like it was filled with library paste. I wondered if she'd fall apart. I looked at Tom. He was sweating; so was I. It made it just that much harder to maintain a grip. I was also having trouble keeping a grip on myself. I saw people with poles running onto the docks across the way. I could tell they were screaming with excitement, but no sound came through.

I forced myself to breathe, to concentrate, to think of the next step.

A blue missed the turn, whizzed between Tom and me.

I gripped Ann's arm with both hands. "Tom," I

yelled. He didn't move. I stamped the dock, tugged Ann's arm. "Tom! Pull! Pull!" He came awake and leaned into it.

As her heels cleared the edge, Tom fell and dropped the rope. Ann slipped from my hands and sagged to the iron plating. Water ran from her mouth and ears and the corners of her eyes; blue in life, they now matched the cracked gray paint of the dock under her. Only in her sodden hair did the new sun spark flashes of life.

Tom's dinghy drifted into my vision, half swamped and churning with more little fish that had overshot the turn. In the middle of the marina a glittering gyre of panicked bait-fish spun, and the big blues sliced into them. Bloody bits and pieces floated to the surface. Gulls screeched onto them. Screaming kids and yelling adults threw lines with bare hooks into the crackling water and the blues snapped them up.

The frenzy built. There were moments when everything seemed airborne—hooks, gulls, lures, little fish, big fish. A huge black and white beauty of a blue soared up, snapping at a gull.

Then, on an unseen signal, the pack of bluefish swerved for the breakwaters and rippled out into the sound.

TOM AND I WERE still on our butts, and for a few moments more we just sat there. On the other side of the basin, a boy and a girl were dragging a big blue by its tail fins, its head bobbing as it crossed the gaps in the dock's planking. Two of the charter boat skippers had hauled Tom's dinghy out and one was scooping bait fish into a red bucket while the other lay flat on the dock to retrieve a floating oar. A fair number of the live-aboards were standing in their cockpits or fore-decks, shielding their eyes from the sun, gazing our way. Some had cell phones out.

I looked at Tom.

He had his arms up and away from himself as though blood, not water, was dripping from them.

I looked at Ann.

She had no shoes. Her right foot was bare; a couple of flies dropped down onto it. The other foot wore a green sock with a letter "S" in white. Her legs were fat and sleek, as though they had somehow been inflated. So too was the rest of her.

Her shirt was bulging at the seams, though still mostly tucked into a gray skirt. Through the wet shirt, she grotesquely overflowed her lacy bra. Her eyes were deeply sunk in her puffy face. But for the strawberry birthmark stark on her neck and bared now to the world, I wouldn't have known her.

Flies were zipping in by dozens and I saw yellow jackets among them. There'd soon be more. Three settled around her eyes; I brushed them off. The sight of them made me frantic. I scrambled to my feet.

"Tom, I'll go for a blanket to cover her."

"Okay, Hade."

"Hang on, Tom. Keep the flies off her."

He gave me a wan smile and a weary thumbs-up. "Can do."

THREE

I HAD BARELY POINTED a toe toward my boat when a Heyoka police car pulled up next to the footbridge that spans the cut between Arkady Island and the mainland. No siren, only twittering red and blue lights.

A dark-clad young woman hopped out of the driver's side. Leaving the stuttering lights on, she strode onto the bridge, all the while talking on a cell phone. She spotted us and held up her unoccupied hand, palm outward in the universal gesture of 'hold everything.'

I looked at Tom. He shrugged, "She's a rookie. A cousin from Flyaway, Mary Devereux."

The fledgling officer arrived at the top of the ramp to the docks and worked her way down, hanging onto the rail with one hand, the phone with the other, and placing her low-heeled shoes deliberately from one traction slat to the next.

Stepping onto the dock, she slapped the phone closed, slipped it into her jacket and strode to Ann.

"Oh, Mother Sea," she said, and pulled her face away. She drew a handkerchief from her pocket and held it over her mouth and nose as, eyes wide, she faced me. "How horrible."

We gazed at each other a moment; her cheekbones were so high they made sills under her eyes. She really did look very young.

She took a couple of breaths, put her handkerchief away and held up her ID card. It showed her in a standard light-blue uniform shirt. Today she was wearing a loose creamy blouse. Her color was deeper, and her black hair a great deal shorter.

She returned her attention to Ann.

"Is she Ann Summerlune-Bullard?"

The fact that she used "she" instead of "this" or "that" in her question softened me.

"Yes," I said.

"How do you know for sure?"

"By the strawberry mark on her neck," I said, with a gesture toward Ann.

"That's what they told me from headquarters, all right." The young Sergeant was rapidly regaining her aplomb and now gave me a quite professional eye. "I guess you knew her pretty well?"

"We were in high school together," I said. We were also what was then referred to as "steadies," but I decided I'd keep that to myself. Several yellow jackets were sidling around on Ann's ear; a few more on the livid blot beneath. The sight made me itch all over and rage began to rise in me again. "I'm getting a blanket to cover her," I said and turned toward my boat.

"I'm afraid that'll have to wait till the coroner's seen her."

My stomach clenched tight as a fist about to strike, but I managed a controlled answer, "Sergeant, a dozen kids go by here on their way to school."

She glanced at her watch, a silver circle on a slender wrist. "It's still early. We'll be done before anyone has to leave for school."

She looked at Ann. "You shouldn't have moved the body, you know."

Again, my stomach knotted; this time I didn't manage to answer quite so evenly. "Sergeant, for heaven's sake, she was out in the middle of the water." I snapped my arm toward the basin and with my temperature rising, went on, "We didn't know it was a body until we got there."

Her chin came up and she said, "Doesn't matter. You should have left it and come in and phoned us."

I was shaky with the effort of staying clamped down, but I managed to keep coherent as I told her about the bluefish. I pointed as a dying baitfish flapped feebly by, most of its tail and belly missing. "Look at that and look at the oily film on the water."

As she turned to look, I felt the first tendrils of the morning breeze on my neck and I backed a few paces into the fresher air. Unconsciously, the Sergeant followed me.

She is awfully young, I thought. What the hell, she's just trying to do what she's been taught. I drew a breath and my stomach eased a millimeter, but I talked with clenched teeth, "If we'd left her, it would have been a horror." Scenes of tangled water, bones and blood flickered through my mind and I felt myself sway.

"Oh, I know," she said. "This must be terribly hard for you." She looked at Tom and I could tell she was also aware of his state. "And for Tom." She put a hand on my arm and said softly, "Even so you should have left it to us."

How could anyone stay angry with someone as decent as this? My stomach eased off and I felt my red rage sliding into gray sorrow. "If we hadn't known her, we might have. But Ann…we couldn't leave her."

Mary Devereaux kept her hand on my arm a moment longer, then removed it and spoke to both of us, "I don't suppose you noticed whether her other sock was on when you found her? Or shoes?"

"I didn't," I said with a sinking feeling. "I'm sorry." Tom just shook his head.

Again she touched my arm. "Oh, it's probably no to both questions."

She let things settle for a minute, then took a black notebook and a silver pen from separate pockets of her jacket and turning brisk, said, "Now, I know Tom; we're related." She poised her pen, "You are?"

"Hadrian Wallace," I said, and it seemed to me she

hesitated for just an instant before she wrote. "And where do you live?"

I pointed to my boat. "There. *Hussar*."

She ran her gaze the long length of my waterborne home and then pointed with her pen to my other boat, moored astern. "Is that little sailboat yours too? It's painted the same shades of green and ivory."

"Yes it is," I said.

"What do you do?"

"I inspect boats for insurance companies; and I write."

She stared at me and she blinked. "Oh, I know you…" She paused, "Ah, well, I know of you, but I thought you were…" She stopped and I watched her color deepen to the shade of her ID photo. I was pretty sure I knew what had flustered her.

Some while ago I did a special service for the nation. It was supposed to be kept quiet, but since it involved several police officers I always felt some sort of story must be in circulation. Hearing that tale—probably at the academy or possibly today on her cell phone—she had assumed I was Heyoka, and I am. But I look white. I take after my mother, a Scot. The only evident red in me is my hair and my freckles. Being very light is not all that uncommon in Heyoka. As a matter of fact, Ann's father was white.

Now I put my hand on her arm. "It's okay," I said.

Mary Devereaux gave me a quick, shy smile, and I

lifted my hand. She turned away, scanned the sky, took a breath, then lifted her notebook again.

"And when did you last see Mrs. Bullard alive?"

"About three weeks ago," I said.

"Why?"

"Why not? She and her husband have a boat here."

"Which one is it?"

"The gray boat with the drooping snout and '77' painted on the bow. Over there." I pointed and her eyes widened as she took it in.

"But that looks like a World War Two PT boat."

"It is."

"Why would anyone want a thing like that?"

I shrugged. "It's the latest fad of the super-rich."

At this point Tom said, "Maybe I'll go make some coffee or something?" and started to walk away.

"Tom, please just stand right there."

"Sure, sure, Mary. How'd you get here so fast, anyway?"

"A 911 call. Said two terrorists were mining the marina. She flipped a couple of pages in her book. "From Alice Emeu."

Tom and I looked at each other and couldn't help wry smiles. "Mining the harbor! That's Alice all over."

"Other people phoned also" said Mary. I had a constant update all the way here." She continued and her face saddened as she spoke, "At first they thought it was just routine...why they sent me, I guess. Then, as

I drove, more reports came in and it got worse. Finally..." she paused and looked at me, "the worst."

There was nothing to say.

A gull planed by, banked, eyed Ann, caught my enraged glare, squawked and flapped off. Mary Devereaux said, "I'll see Alice Emeu and these others later." She surveyed the silent onlookers and as she turned back to us, her coat swung open and I saw a revolver in black leather.

"Now," she said, raising her notebook again, "tell me why you two were up and about so early."

Tom said he was working at his shop to finish a boat for a customer who was coming from Boston to pick it up. Done, he walked down to the harbor for a breather, spotted something odd in the water and, seeing my light, came to *Hussar*. I told her about my book deadline. She made a few swift notes, flipped the book closed, slid it into a pocket, hesitated and then said, "Neither of you should leave Heyoka without letting me know."

I looked at Tom. He looked at me. We both stared at his cousin.

I recovered first. "Why in the world...?"

Mary Devereaux glanced over at Ann. "You are material witnesses in a death." And possibly more deeply implicated, was what the police academy had trained her to think. But, of course, that she could not and did not say.

Before she or we could say any more, our attention was taken by a convoy of warbling official vehicles that swept into the parking lot and halted by Sergeant Devereaux's car.

"Wait here," she said, "while I have a word with the coroner and the other guys."

Ogod, if I have to stay on my feet another second, I'll keel over.

FOUR

AS USUAL IN HEYOKA, the "other guys" were mostly female. Five people appeared from the three vehicles: two husky young women in blue and an older woman with a camera bag; a middle aged, mustached man in tan who wheeled a gurney and white body bag across the bridge; a large rotund lady in a dark green dress and white coat who poured from the door of a yellow station wagon and flowed onto the bridge in a cloud of cigarette smoke.

"Good grief," I said, "It's Moby Woman."

"Coroner, I guess," said Tom.

She and the Sergeant met in the middle of the span, put their heads together. At one point, Mary Devereaux fished out her notebook and waved it in our direction while the big woman lit a cigarette.

"How do you and your cousin get along, Tom?"

Tom took my meaning and smiled, "Oh, she's really okay, Hade. She's just young and trying very hard."

"I'll say. If she doesn't watch out, next thing you know, she'll be a lieutenant."

Tom grinned and looked a little more normal as we

stood there, shooing bees and swatting flies, and waiting for the conference on the bridge to end.

At last, the ovoid lady dropped her coffin nail and mashed it under a white sneaker.

Moving very fast for something so big, the coroner surged down the ramp and wheezed to a stop alongside Tom. She was shorter than he, but darn near as wide. Her hair was a pulled into a single black braid, thick as a club. Her brown eyes bulged.

"You two found her?"

"Yes, Ma'am," we confessed.

She grabbed Tom's arm, lowered herself to her knees and opened her bag. The huge lady's hands were dainty with unlacquered nails. She snapped on a pair of latex gloves, lifted Ann's right arm, let it fall; looked briefly into the blank eyes, then closed them. She picked up the sockless foot and tested the motion of the ankle. She took Ann's head in her hands and probed with her fingers and thumbs as though she were checking a melon for soft spots. She pulled back the collar of Ann's shirt. I guessed she was trying to see how far the birth mark went.

The mark runs from the right side of her neck and across her back onto her left buttock. I used to tell Ann it was where an angel had cradled her before she was born. The coroner didn't need to hear this from me, though. She'd soon know more about Ann than anyone except the angels.

Moby Woman turned her attention to her colleagues who had filed unnoticed onto the dock.

"Okay, Mabel, take pictures. Then you two kids get her into the bag and help Mike with the trolley. Michael, I'll see you back at the morgue."

"Yes, Miz Meadowlark." they answered in a chorus.

Miz Meadowlark hoisted herself to her feet on Tom's arm and walked us aside so Mabel could get to work. She looked at us, "You can go now."

"Yes ma'am," Tom and I said together.

She paused to light another cigarette and, trailing smoke and ash, undulated away toward her car.

Tom looked at me and I looked at him. Awed, we gazed after her.

"Holy smoke," said Tom.

I didn't know whether he intended the pun on smoke or not, and I was too weary to care. "Just so, partner, just so," I said and gave him a pat on the shoulder.

Mabel set a video camera on a tripod and took a slow pan of the entire marina. Then she took out an ornate digital camera and carefully photographed Ann's body from all angles, taking more than one shot at each angle. She also did the dock, the dinghy and the view from the deck of *Hussar* where Tom and I had whispered in the dawn. I saw those pictures a long time later and we both looked about as dead as Ann.

With the photographic record made Mabel packed her gear, the young women zipped Ann into the white sack. They carried her up the ramp, stretched her out on the gurney and the lone male wheeled her across the bridge where the three of them loaded her into the van.

She was gone.

FIVE

As I once again turned toward my brine-borne home, the first of the children who lived on boats in the marina began to pass by on their way to school.

They were in their standard blue and white uniforms, virtually every one wearing a knapsack with the Heyoka logo on it—a full moon behind an oil derrick spouting a rainbow. The girls were walking in pairs, holding hands, darting glances at us and the place where Ann had been; the boys went mostly one by one. They looked like a file of Sherpas tramping provisions into the high Himalayas. Here and there, a few adults still kept the deck, those to the east black silhouettes; those to the west hands to their brows as though saluting the sun.

"Where's the dinghy?" asked Tom.

I pointed across the basin.

Tom said, "I'll get it later," and he trudged off toward Gretchen.

I plodded to *Hussar,* watched a gull drop a clam onto the concrete slab at the inner end of the west breakwater. It bounced; another gull swooped in, snatched it.

The sky was blue, the sun was gold. Eskar Island Sound glittered.

Hell of a day to be dead.

I slumped into the pilot house, intending to sit down and mull things over while absorbing a little vodka—maybe a lot of vodka. The marina was astir now. A few people came by, curious, but once they had a look at me, turning away.

I crept below.

My mind was mud, my eyes itched and my ears were ringing.

How could Ann be dead?

I thought about a shower. Too much effort. Dragging on dry clothes was all I could manage. I washed my hands and face in the galley sink, hoisted a bottle of vodka from the liquor locker, dropped a handful of cubes in the tumbler from the dawn, filled it, drank half. It was crisp. It stung. It felt great.

I added a few more cubes and refilled. I went to my cabin and scanned the CD rack. My hand reached for *Musick on the Death of Queen Mary*—Henry Purcel's flat-out shriek of rage and pain. No…too strong…the wrenching thud of that drum! I couldn't take it. My hand moved to *Pavanne for a Dead Princess*. Good…Ravel for four guitars…largo, elegiac, lyrical…but no. Lovely responsible steady Ann was no princess. My hand moved on to *Sopranos' Favorite Mozart Arias*. I plucked the CD up and scanned the list of songs…

Dove' Sono...a mature woman grieves vanished joy. Perfect. The silver disk whispered into the player and I poked the buttons to play the aria again and again, a dozen times over.

A muted pop; the speakers hissed. A shining voice streamed forth, took wing, implored Heaven: *"Dove sono?"*—Where has my life gone?

Where indeed.

SIX

A BRIGHT RED FISH SWAM in black water. It turned into a red sock…the sock was swallowed by a white letter "P"…the letter unfolded and was a woman with long black hair and she weaved away through the dark water like a pale snake…

I woke up sweating and feeling sick. The vodka-over-ice I had poured for myself when I got back to *Hussar* was gone, the empty tumbler on its side by my hand. The cabin was stuffy and hot. I had forgotten to turn on the air conditioner.

I remembered pouring the drink and putting on a CD, but not much beyond that. The player had turned itself off, but the speakers were hissing.

By the clock on the bulkhead and the light in the portholes, it was going on one in the afternoon. My stomach felt like a gravel pit and the area behind my eyebrows hurt. My nerves were strung as tight as the rigging on my sailboat.

How many drinks had I had, anyway? Was this still Thursday or had I slept the clock around?

I eyed the toppled tumbler and the damp spot where

the ice had melted, and my stomach squirmed. I put the glass on the floor and studied the underside of the deck for a moment; the white paint was distinctly gray and I saw a flaking spot. God, another chore. It was endless. Maybe I should move ashore? No, houses were even more work and you couldn't go anywhere in them.

With a sigh and a throbbing behind my eyes, I creaked to my feet and shuffled aft to check the day on my fax machine...still Thursday. Feeling a little more alive, I went back to my cabin and, standing on the bed, looked out at the marina.

It was drowsing away under the high sun of summer, the boats and pilings rippling in the air rising from the hot docks. The only signs of life were two men stacking white plastic bags onto the side deck of Frank Bullard's boat. Supplies for a weekend party, I supposed. That was about all Frank Bullard had done with the boat so far. Word was she didn't have engines...

A party and Ann not buried? Not possible, even to a horse's ass like Frank Bullard.

I shrugged, opened all the portholes in the cabin, and shed my clothes. A hot shower would purge the nightmare and ease my nerves...but the feel of the soap startled me. It reminded me of Ann's cold, slippery arm. I got the bottle of detergent from the galley and used that instead.

Afterwards, I put on all clean clothes, right down

to a pair of virtually new loafers. I was hoping I could leave the events of this day's dawn with my old clothing, that the smell and feel of clean duds would erase the gray from my spirits the way the hot water had drowned the dream.

An infusion of our national soul food—corn chowder made smooth and thick and creamy—would probably help, but first I had to get into town. I made a cup of coffee, dropped in three aspirins, laced it with milk and bourbon, and sipped at it while I slowly climbed the stairs to the pilot house.

As I got there, the two men I had seen at Frank Bullard's boat passed by, pushing two-wheeled carts. I watched them as they walked across the bridge, put the carts into a tan panel truck and drove away. It was a lot like my final sight of Ann.

I poked through the drawers under the settee until I found a heavy-duty mailer for the corrected pre-pub copy of my book I'd been working on at dawn.

Did everything happen this morning?... Only seven or so hours ago? My God, it seemed another age.

I was lucky to have finished the work before Tom arrived and I was soothed by the simple chore of stuffing the floppy wad of paper into the heavy envelope and stapling it shut. I tucked it under my arm, and set an exploratory foot onto the dock.

The gray planking was scorching, so I walked awkwardly back on the heels of my thin-soled shoes, until

I got to the bridge. The planking here was unpainted and much more comfortable underfoot. The tide was out and the briny smell of weed and wet rock was strong on the humid air.

As I was walking along the road to town, a streetcar glided alongside and slowed to my pace. It was one of the new ones with air conditioning and the driver whom I had known since my teens, gave me a smile and a sign to hop aboard. This was the section of town where no vehicles, not even bikes were allowed, so I stepped out into the street and returned her smile, but said I needed the walk and waved her on. I was sweating a little, but I didn't want to get into a conversation about Ann. With a flip of her hand, the driver shoved the control handle forward and the glossy yellow machine whispered away so smoothly I could hear the blue sparks buzzing on its pantograph.

The new stainless steel doors of the old brick post office were wedged fully open, but the lobby was stuffy. I knew the clerks, a husky blond and a lean old Heyoka woman, but not on a first name basis. I could tell they were curious, but they were also too polite to initiate a conversation, so I was able to pay and watch in silence as the labor of two years was dropped into a grimy mail sack. It reminded me of Ann Bullard going into her penultimate package. Well, hers at least had been new and white and antiseptically clean.

Done at the post office, I walked on toward the *Hic*

& Ubique convenience store at the corner. I scanned the store through the windows, but saw no one I knew.

I wandered the aisles, but nothing appealed to me except a fresh bottle of vodka. Then I had to wait while an elderly woman presented a pink check to the cashier and he opened the register, counted out and laid down several hundred dollars. The lady counted the money again, put it in her purse and left. Years ago I'd regularly done the same thing for my mother—turned one of those pink rectangles of paper from the Common Wealth of Heyoka into cash. They were about the only things more ubiquitous than the "Ubiquay" stores themselves.

I paid for my *eau-de-vie* and saw by the sun that I could reasonably show up at the Papageno Café for a late lunch. I loved the Papageno.

The original stainless steel diner had been built in Paterson, New Jersey, around 1930 and, according to a plate on the steam table, and was "Silk City Special No. 901." Over the years a cluster of small buildings and dining rooms were added and were now haphazardly linked together, some by full corridors, some with simple roofed breezeways. There were rooms with fireplaces, rooms with blackboards, rooms with arcade games; there was a bar, saloon style, and there was a bar, piano style; there was a wood shingled building with newspapers, magazines and a freewheeling library that worked on the principle of take-one-leave-one. In one corner there was a coffee urn with a very unbusiness-like bowl full of change and bills for customers to pay or not pay for the coffee, make change or steal a little. It was supposedly emptied twice a day, but whenever I looked at it, it was always full.

The entire melange was a cozy, ramshackle maze and had the only eateries near the marina. It rambled over a low hill with a fine view of the sound and Arkady Island. The place had been in the Summerlune family for generations and was evidently named Papageno after a character in one of Mozart's operas, though nobody knew why. Anyway, I had started eating there when it was on cinder blocks and had yet to be poisoned.

Henry Lightfoot, cook and mainstay of the place, came out as I gratefully stepped into the air conditioning. There were only a few other people, most chatting over mugs of coffee; thankfully, no one I recognized.

Henry looked somber and said, "I heard about this morning; real sad. I saw you and Tom out there in the dinghy. Then those blues." He paused as though watching it play over again in his mind. "Real touch and go, wasn't it?" He gave me a sympathetic pat on the shoulder.

I was inclined to tell Henry that the police thought we should have left things alone, but before I could, he grabbed me lightly by the other shoulder and aimed me at a corner booth.

"Go sit down. What you need is a bowl of corn chowder."

I grinned a grin of relief, "Henry, you are a prince."

"Hey, Wallace," he said, "Around here I am king," and he swaggered through the swinging doors into the kitchen.

I looked down at the marina and saw Frank Bullard emerge from the cabin of his boat. A rectangular block of a man, he was dressed for the city, dark suit, lavender shirt, red tie. He stooped and it looked like he was locking the cabin door.

Jesus, I hope he's not coming up here.

Out on the sound, way over by Eskar Island I could see dark areas on the water—a breeze ruffling in from the southwest.

My chowder came and I kept one eye on Frank Bullard while I took in the rich aroma and waited for it to cool. By the time the chowder was the right temperature, Bullard had crossed the bridge and driven off. I relaxed and drove my spoon into the thick porridge and forgot all about him.

When I had finished the chowder and my second cup of coffee, the sun was sliding into late afternoon and more and more people were ambling into the Papageno. Sooner or later there was bound to be someone I couldn't duck. I left enough money on the table to cover things, grabbed my plain brown package and waved goodbye to Henry through the porthole in the kitchen door.

I paused in the middle of the footbridge to watch the now-flooding tide rippling over the rocks below and to take deep breaths of cool fresh brine.

A small plane purred overhead, slanting down toward the airstrip at the far end of the island. It hung for an instant like a crucifix. Then the sun swallowed it.

Ann had loved the Papageno too.

SEVEN

THE NEXT DAY was Friday the thirteenth, but it began pretty well anyway.

The sky was without cloud, the wind easy. It looked like the breeze would fill in from the southwest, the sky would turn smoky and Eskar Island would turn blue and disappear in haze.

I went below and made another cup of coffee and climbed back up to lean against the dark, cool paneling of the pilot house. Framed in the doorway, was the bow of Frank Bullard's boat, *Taurus*. Perched right on the stemhead, was a seagull rooting gingerly among its tail feathers. Might be the one the blue had snapped at yesterday.

The red pennant on the rail above the gull flapped and I went on deck to look out into the sound. The wind was coming in from the southwest and it was getting hazy. Already, Eskar Island looked like a whale sliding into a fog bank.

As walked back toward the pilot house I saw the mail-lady leave the marina office and also noticed a long-standing friend of Ann's and of mine, Arianna Lencouvert, poised at the top of the ramp.

I had seen Arianna at irregular intervals over the years since we were all in high school together, and to me she always looked exactly the way she had back then. Well, a little fuller around the edges, maybe, but if anything that was an improvement.

She saw me, waved, descended the ramp and walked carefully across the slick plating of the fuel dock. She swung into a more confident stride as she reached the wooden walkway.

She was wearing a cream-colored dress that rippled in the gathering breeze. Her hair was pulled straight back and held with a scarf of the same material; strands of her long black hair flickered in the wind. Around her neck was a thin chain of gold.

A few guys came out of the cabins of their sport-fishermen and begin to fiddle around with hoses and mops as she passed. Their eyes were not on their work.

She halted by the boarding platform to *Hussar*'s deck, shaded her eyes with a hand and said, "Hi, Hadrian." She was now close enough for me to see the small vertical gap between her front teeth.

"Hi yourself, stranger. Come aboard," and I held out my hand. She took it and I led her out of the sun and into the shade of the pilot house.

"Get you a cup of coffee? A drink?" I realized I

was still holding her hand and let go, feeling a little off balance.

Arianna didn't seem to mind. She lifted the hand I had held and ran it over her forehead, smoothing hair that needed absolutely no attention as far as I could tell. Her brown eyes had a twinkle and she showed me the gap in her teeth again.

"A soda would be nice. Something with ice if you have it." She sat down on one end of the settee.

"Dockside, we've got ice. And air conditioning, and a telephone. Underway, what we've mostly got is lots of hot water," I replied as I went down the five steps to the galley.

"Oh? Why is that?"

"*Hussar* runs on steam."

"She doesn't look like a steamboat," said Arianna. "More like a submarine; so long and slender. I like the color of the hull and house, though. Just about matches my dress. Is it proper to call a boat named *Hussar* 'she' by the way?"

"Well, I do," I said. "Besides, a hussar is a fish as well as a cavalryman and this Hussar was probably named for the fish. Her sister ships were called *Gar, Pike, Muskellunge* and *Barracuda*." I came up the stairs and handed her a glass of ginger ale.

"I see" she said. "All the long skinny ones. Well, that's apt. And where did you find her?"

I grinned at this because I literally had *found* my

boat—in the Bahamas, awash and abandoned up a muddy tidewater slough "Up a creek on Andros Island," I said.

"With this beautiful paneling?"

"Oh no, she was pretty much bare metal everywhere, plain as a pikestaff. I'm pretty sure she was a rum-runner back in the twenties…there are dents on the aft side of the pilot house I'm nearly certain are from bullets. She had three engines when I found her. With all that power she'd have been very fast for her time. Tom Sorrell and I did the paneling. He made this steering wheel."

I realized I was chattering and stepped away from the circle of laminated spruce and mahogany I'd been leaning on and eased into a canvas deck chair by the doorway.

"Tom went with you to the Bahamas?"

"Yes. And another friend. Steve Holm. I don't think you know him. He's only been here about a year. It was Tom's boat we made the trip in."

Arianna leaned forward and the gold chain swayed from her skin about an inch and I got a sense of just how nicely she had filled out over the years. She moved the glass to her other hand and I watched a drop of water run down and pool on the inside of her thumb.

"Are you very upset about Ann?" The light streaming in through the front windows of the pilot house made dots of her pupils. There were tiny flecks of gold in the brown irises.

"Well..." I was tempted to deflect Arianna. But, hell, there was no hope of that. Ann was one class ahead of Arianna and me. Our senior year, Ann had gone off to college and I'd gone off my rocker, written her several snide and cutting letters and the relationship had dissolved.

Years later and quite by chance Ann and I had been part of the crew on a transatlantic passage. It had been a slow trip, light winds during the day, calms at night. Sharing nightwatches, we'd talked things over, laughed about my abysmal behavior and rediscovered a mutual affection. She'd forgiven me with a hug and said, "What we are is shipmates. Always have been, really." Then, gazing at the glowing sweep of stars, she'd murmured, "That other stuff fades, but shipmates, you know, are forever."

There was really no way I could fool Arianna, so I just confessed it plain: "Yes. Yes I am." I took a big swig of coffee and told her about my dream and she listened intently, sitting forward on the settee.

"You know," I concluded, "beyond the shock, it bothers me that she was shoeless, and that one sock was missing."

"Go on"

"Well, you know, Ann was quite athletic. When we were racing..." I gestured astern toward my sailboat,

"...she used to set the spinnaker by herself. Damn few people can do that, Ari. I fell overboard the two times I tried it."

Arianna threw back her head and laughed, "I never heard that before."

"Yeah," I said, a little embarrassed that I'd let it slip even now, "it's not something I brag about. Anyway, I just don't see her accidentally falling into the water. Besides, in the water she was an otter."

Arianna said, "Maybe she fell in because she was getting into her shoes and socks. You know, hopping around on one leg; something like that?"

"Why in the world would she be doing that. You don't exactly go wading around here. It's all rocks, weed and barnacles; slimy, slippery and sharp."

"They could have come off while she was in the water. There's no telling how far the currents could have dragged her."

"Oh, I suppose," I grumbled, and stared at the tepid black dregs in my cup.

Arianna reached out and put her hand on mine. "Wait and see what the police decide."

She lifted her hand away and took a sip of soda and eyed me over the rim of the glass, cocking her head to one side, birdlike. It popped into my mind that the Heyoka words "Arian na" mean "bright wing" or "little bird."

"Did I hear you've done another book about another Renaissance rakehell?"

"Guilty," I admitted with what I hoped was a modest smile. After all, I was talking with the author of a string of best sellers.

"Who is it this time?"

"A real wild man named do Floreados. Alfonso do Floreados. It means flourish." I poked out a leg, bowed deep and wove my arm around in arabesques.

Arianna laughed. "Was that really his name?"

"One of them," I said. "He changed names every time he married. And he lived a long time—one hundred and thirteen years—and married often."

Arianna shook her head. "Good heavens!"

"Exactly. When he got tired of one, he poisoned her and moved on." I waited a moment and saw I had Ari's eyes wide before I said, "Fittingly, his last wife—Fredrieka von Hohenscharfzahn—poisoned him."

"Great Mother Sea, Hadrian, you may have a seller here."

"Sure be nice," I said. We looked at the other with the pleasant camaraderie the contemplation of wealth induces.

Arianna took a quick swallow from her glass and asked, "What else did this horror do?" then grinned and added, "Not that he had to do much else."

"He forged a Rembrandt." Arianna's eyes really went wide at this, and I quickly added, "At least that's what I think. It's a hot topic in the art world."

"Is it a well known painting?"

"Oh, yes," I said. "The Polish Rider."

"The huge one at the Frick in New York? The kid on the creaky old horse?" She stood, put her arm on her hip and thrust her elbow forward. The kid's got his elbow stuck way out?"

"That's it," I affirmed. "I loved it the instant I saw it. It's every teenage boy with his first car."

Arianna grinned and let out another rippling laugh. She put her glass down, took my head between her hands and planted a kiss on my brow. "Oh, Hadrian, "I can't wait to read it!"

Her enthusiasm and her kiss just about unhinged me. I was glad I was sitting. "Well, thanks for the blessing, Ari." I said the book was "in the mail" and she laughed, and we beamed at each other for a long moment until my wits returned. It was high time to turn from me to her.

"How is it you're in town?" I asked.

"I'm moving into the old lighthouse on Hammerclaw Point." She pointed toward the east end of the island where the old light's windows showed above the trees.

"I had no idea."

"It's been rather sudden. My Oregon publisher was bought by a Japanese company, and my editor didn't want to stay. She moved to New York, so I had no reason to stay out there." She put her fingers on her forehead, smoothing her flawless hairline and as the material of her dress rose with her arm, I got a hint of the heft underneath.

"Hadrian, I've got to go to the lighthouse now. They're painting. But I want to talk some more. I'll call you in a day or two, if that's all right?"

"Of course." I got up and handed her down the steps of the boarding platform. This time when she smiled I could see fine tracery radiating from the corners of her eyes, the mark of all who grow up around the water. She gave a wave and turned toward the footbridge.

If Arianna filled her blouse sweetly, walking away she was truly winsome. As she crossed the bridge, it was evident that the swabbing fishermen agreed. Old do Floreados had written a fair amount of verse on the subject of the well-turned female bottom—*Odes to Callipygia.* I'd have to look them up.

I was also reminded of something else cynical Alf wrote in his journal, "When a woman says nice things about your home, oil the hinges on the back door."

Well, if Arianna had romance in mind, I was young enough to be interested—and old enough to wait.

Or was I?

Was I really over Ann? Had I ever been? Would I ever be?

Whatever I was, Arianna would sense it—she wouldn't push.

Or would she?

I shrugged. No matter. It was academic. In Heyoka, the women make the moves.

EIGHT

BE SURE YOUR SINS will find you out.

I was standing there, continuing my analysis of Arianna's sashay when a boat horn screeched. I turned around and saw Steve Holm's yawl, *Buzzard,* coming through the gap between the stone breakwaters. Out of the corner of my eye, I saw Arianna turn, shade her eyes with both hands for a moment and then walk on across the bridge to the parking lot.

I'd had a postcard from Steve the day before Tom and I discovered Ann. He was leaving Bermuda and would probably make his usual midnight arrival in five or six days; so I shouldn't wait up. His comment had given me a chuckle at the time and it made me smile now. It was true—somehow or another, no matter how long or short the trip, Steve Holm always arrived in the wee hours. After he took up residence in the marina, we had made several deliveries together, taking boats south to Florida and the Virgin Islands in the winter, then bringing them back north in the spring. We invariably got where we were going in the dead of night, and usually facing the additional task of snaking a deep-draft sailboat up a shallow unlighted channel at dead low water.

Well, Steve had clearly had an unusual passage and was going to make port in daylight despite all historical precedents and current expectations.

Steve was at the wheel, bare-headed, wearing his usual summer outfit of white tee-shirt and yellow swim trunks. It looked like he had given up shaving since he left, and his beard was bushy, black and ragged. Although he owned his boat outright and was a widely read columnist, he looked like a total bum; something he would have been glad to hear, because that was the exactly what he wanted everyone to think. Steve divided the world into "strivers" and "workers" and he preferred to keep his distance from the strivers.

I waved and he raised a hand from the steering wheel. I trotted around to his slip and he handed me the stern and aft spring lines as *Buzzard* glided into her slot. He hopped off with the bow line and forward spring and we wove the four ropes around their cleats and cinched them up, my lines twanging and creaking as they brought the boat to a full stop.

Steve looked weary. His brown eyes seemed to take things in kind of slowly; the whites were noticeably bloodshot. Apparently he'd made the passage alone.

"Rough trip?" I asked.

"No, not really. Just long. No wind from the Gulf

Stream on, and the autopilot broke. Lot of time under power and a lot of steering."

He looked idly around the marina for a moment and ran both hands through his hair which was wind blown and sticking up, down and sideways.

"Think I need a haircut?"

"Nope," I said. "A couple of quarts of used crank-case oil and a pitch fork should fix it up just fine."

He grinned and said: "Anything interesting happen around here while I was gone or are you just sitting around as usual, listening to the seagulls fart?"

I told him about Ann.

His gaze rested on me for a long moment, and I saw some of my distress emerge in his expression of deepening concern.

"You mean the lively little power-walker with the long black hair who wears the port and starboard socks?"

"Yes, I said. "Yes, that's her."

Steve stroked his beard for a long moment. "Have they scheduled the inquiry?"

"If they have, I haven't heard about it."

"You'd hear about it. You would have to appear. You and Tom and anyone else around at the time. Probably be next week. I'll see what I can find out when I get the phone and computer plugged in."

He scanned the central basin and the fuel dock, "Come below while I hack off the shrubbery."

With him in the head compartment with the door open and me on the settee in the cabin, he ran hot water into the sink, rubbed the mirror and said, "Well, that's the bad news. Anything good happen?"

"Arianna's back, and she's bought the old Hammerclaw lighthouse. She's fixing it up to live in."

"Arianna Lencouvert? The writer?" In the mirror, I could see his eyebrows rising. "The one who does those 800-page Pleistocene Panters you're always reading? *Erika the Red,* et al?" He bent and worked hot water into his beard. He paused and looked at me in the mirror. "Oh ho, she was the lady on the bridge. God, how many books are there, anyway?"

"There are six, Steve, and, yes, that is she."

Steve's eyes went wide and he mouthed 'That is she' as he started working in the lather.

"Hadrian, honestly, how do you do it? Every summer some exotic number cruises through here and you're like a minnow before a blue. Chomp!" He made a snapping mouth with one sudsy hand.

"Hey, you've only been here two summers."

"Hey, nothing. You've told me about other times; times before I moved up here. Last year it was that upper-crust Portuguese flake, Conchita..."

"Her name is Consuela," I said.

"Consuela, Conchita. What's the difference? Next year I'm gong to stay here and take a course at Heyoka U., too. God knows, my love life's nothing to rave about."

I laughed. "If you ever call Consuela 'Conchita,' you'll hear a lot of vivid Portuguese and may not have much left for love."

He grinned at me through the suds and said into the mirror, "No doubt, brother. I remember well you two's set-to's."

"Wait..." He held up the razor. "Now what did she call them? Ah, yes, 'lessons in temperament.'"

"Yeah. Well, I gave as good as I got."

"'Deed you did, Hade." He made several sweeping strokes. "You held the usual untenable male positions most staunchly. Indeed you did."

Besides," I said, "this isn't like that. I've known Arianna a long time."

"Really?"

"In a sense, yes."

"What sense?"

"From grade school on. Arianna was in my high school class, but she went to college out west; ended up in Oregon. Now she's moving into the old light-house, so she may be back for good."

Steve made the final strokes, picked up a towel and said, "Here we go again! It must be your freck-les and beady blue eyes." He started opening and closing lockers, looking, I guessed, for a clean shirt. "Anyway, your hair and the lady's skin are a nice match."

He found and pulled on a green tee-shirt with the

Bermuda islands strung across the chest in a lopsided white 'J', and said, "How do I look?"

"Ann's sock was on the wrong foot."

"What?" said Steve.

"It just occurred to me… I was thinking back to Arianna's visit, remembering how I'd described Ann to her… Then the color of your shirt…and the white islands making a letter…" I shook my head to clear the clutter and drew a fresh breath.

"The green sock was on Ann's left foot." I closed my eyes and brought up the picture of her on the dock. "Yeah… I was on her left side and so was the sock."

"Maybe it was a kind of reverse chic," suggested Steve. "The green starboard-side sock on the left foot where the red port one…" His voice trailed off.

"I've seen her in that outfit many times, Steve; never with the colors reversed."

"Yeah, well, let's see what they make of it at the official inquiry." He lifted a bottle of blue liquid out of a locker and winced as he swabbed on the aromatic aftershave. "Now, to repeat myself, how do I look?"

His face above the lips was a dark suntanned mask, below, deathly white.

"Like a raccoon," I said.

He grinned and studied the mirror. I see what you mean." He put the bottle back in the locker and closed the lid. "By the way, where in Oregon did La Lencouvert live?"

"Salem," I said.

Steve's eyebrows shot up and his grin became wolfish. "Well, well, well. How very apt. The lady's from Witch City."

NINE

WITCH CITY, OF COURSE, is Salem, Massachusetts, not Salem, the capital of Oregon, but I could see Steve was trying to alert me to the perils of another cozy winter of fun and games followed by a lonely spring, and took it as offered, in friendship.

Steve Holm may have mixed up his Salems in fun or to make a point, but he was right about the date of the formal inquiry. Ten days after we'd found Ann, Tom and I went to the courthouse. It was downtown and as yet unhit by the forces of modernization, an 18th Century relic whose bricks no longer ran truly parallel, but rose and fell with gentle sinuosity.

Alice Emeu entered looking like a Heyoka oil well—dark blue dress, red, yellow and green feathers spouting from her gray hair.

The panel was a clutch of seven elderly ladies that called to mind a pack of eager ferrets and in whose wrinkles and white hair, the history of the nation was writ fine.

The woman who presented the results of the official investigation and led the testimony was a sleek young thing in gray and white who stacked an armload of files on a long table in front of the panel. She wore an ornate gold watch and while quizzing each of us she sat on the edge of the table, swinging a shapely leg and turning the watch around and around on her wrist.

Tom and I told our story.

Alice Emeu started to natter on, but was expertly stifled.

Medical Examiner Meadowlark gave her report: Ann had been rendered unconscious by a smack on her forehead and drowned because she was already in the water or subsequently fell into it. Testimony given, she swept up the aisle and out of the room, probing her purse for a fresh cigarette.

The trim young woman in gray continued to build the case that Ann had accidentally drowned, probably during the weekend she was missed and approximately three weeks before Tom and I found her.

It was all very matter-of-fact, until the bereft husband, Frank Bullard was called.

Frank came on, big, bullnecked and bereft, and got progressively more glum the further he went into his story.

Frank said that on the Friday of the weekend she went missing "Candace" (Ann's middle name. Not once in his testimony did Frank Bullard use her first name) left the house a little after dark for her usual evening walk. He drove out to find her and say goodbye because he was taking a flight for the Far East. He caught up with her near the marina. They had walked out on the bridge, talking about this and that, watching the moonrise. He said his wife started dropping coins into the water and he asked her what she was wishing, but she wouldn't tell him. He got a little tearful at this point, but controlled it manfully.

At the mention of coins, I must have jumped a little or given some other sign because I caught a sideways glance from the skipper of *Taurus* and Frank's meaty face shifted toward me.

I looked around the room, first at Tom Sorrell, then at the officials and finally at the other folks sitting with us behind the railing in the witness section. I thought Bullard was lying and expected at least a break in the rhythm of the testimony.

But the paper tape just kept flowing from the stenotype machine and the reels on the tape recorder wheeled on. The seven ladies were still keen but the expressions on many of the faces in the rest of the room ran from mild boredom to terminal ennui. Alice Emeu had actually fallen asleep, her chin down on her chest. She looked like a squat pot of flowers.

Tom and Steve were studying the dusty molding where the upper edges of the walnut paneling met the down-curve of the vaulted ceiling. By showing emotion, Frank had violated the boatmen's code of stoicism in the face of everything and it embarrassed them.

As for me, I was amazed. Frank Bullard's little poetic touch about the moon had given me another anomaly to chew on.

In Eskar Island Sound, when the moon is low, so is the tide. And when the tide is out there isn't a lot of water under the Arkady Island footbridge. Coins can be dropped only onto kelp, rocks, slime and the odd starfish.

When Bullard said he saw the moon rising over Eskar Island, he was saying the tide was out. Water under the bridge and a low moon could not coincide.

Or could they?

I concentrated and pictured the bridge and the cut between the marina and the mainland. I saw pools and puddles under the bridge and, yes, dammit, some of them did last from tide to tide. Minnows and crabs got trapped in them regularly. The gulls ate them or the next tide washed them free. Bullard could have meant Ann was tossing coins into one of those pools.

Several of the ladies on the panel had noticed the skipper's glance at me and the lady in gray had seen Frank's attention shift. She stopped toying with her watch and turned to me, "Do you have something to add, Mr. Wallace?"

Oshit, I thought, I guess I can't challenge him in any convincing way.

"No, ma'am," I said, rather sheepishly, and the young woman turned back to Frank.

Yet, why had there been that sudden shift in Frank's gaze? Perhaps he'd merely been reacting to the look his captain shot at me. The captain may merely have been taking notice of my start.

Logical and reasonable.

I'm not particularly logical or reasonable. I didn't like it. I had a feeling there was more bull to Frank than the beast in his surname and the golden *Taurus* on the transom of his trendy war boat.

But what good is a feeling?

TEN

"DEATH BY MISADVENTURE."

I was reading the story on the front page of the morning edition of the *Heyoka Ear* as Tom, Steve and I sat in the Papageno, sipped orange juice and waited for our coffee to cool and our eggs and bacon to arrive.

Inset into the second paragraph was a picture of Ann. It looked like it was taken about ten years ago. Her hair was adrift on her forehead, so perhaps it was shot out of doors on a windy day. She was holding a tennis racket. She was smiling, so it was definitely before she married Bullard.

I put the paper aside.

"As I get it, the official version is she was wading and generally frisking about on the rocky part of the park across from the east end of Arkady, slipped, conked her head, slid into the water and drowned. Do you think the women on the panel bought that?"

"They have," said Steve and then he paused before saying with emphasis, "For the record. It is conceivable, after all. There is a little beach there, as well as the rocks. She could have gone wading, then been hopping around getting into her socks and shoes and tipped over. Happens all the time. I did it not long ago getting into my sea boots."

Steve buried his nose in his cup, then added wryly, "Besides, it's in print, so it must be true."

I shook my head. "Look, I was watching those biddies pretty carefully and I didn't get the impression they were entirely happy with the explanation of the bruises the examiner found under Ann's clothing."

"That's right," said Tom, "Someone asked how there could be bruises, but not scratches on her arms and legs? Specially since the theory is the body drifted all the way from the park to the marina. That's a lot of dragging by the tide until the gas…" he paused and his eyes darted around, "…you know, until she, er, floated up."

Tom's brow looked a little moist and I suspected he had been about to say "bloated up."

"The marina bottom's basically mud," said Steve. "I've been over the side to clean the centerboard of my boat enough times to know that. Besides, if you're dead you don't bruise."

"How come?" asked Tom and I together.

"No blood pressure," said Steve. "Bruises are made by blood leaking from breaks in veins. No pressure, no leaks. Anyway, that's not the reason the jury bought the story."

"Oh?" said Tom and I again. This was getting to be a habit. First with Miz Meadowlark, now with Steve.

"No. They went along with it because no one suggested a motive for foul play. Everyone close to "Candace"—as Bullard called her-had an alibi. Bullard was in Hong Kong, Ann's mother at home in a house full of servants. You and Tom were on a delivery trip to Nova Scotia. Bullard's skipper was riding shotgun on a truck enroute with the new engines for the PT boat..." He stopped and looked out the window. "Speaking of which, here they are now to take her away."

The three of us followed a dark green tugboat down between the breakwaters, watched it turn and back up to the PT boat. A crewman in blue coveralls and a red watch cap passed the tow hawser to the khaki-clad skipper on the bow. He wove it around the PT's mooring bitts, and the tug hauled *Taurus* away.

"I wonder where they're taking her?"

Without moving his eyes from the window, Tom said, "If they turn east it'll be Flyaway Island, west it'll be Sheldrake Shipyard. Those are the only two places on the sound that can handle a boat her size anymore."

Our breakfasts arrived at this point and we settled down to stoking up. I noticed a cardboard box on the seat next to Tom.

"What's in the box? Roses?" The box was the right size and shape.

Tom laid a hand on the box and grinned, "No, it's a model of Frank Bullard's new tanker."

"Aha! The reason for all the work going on at the

terminal," I said. "Let's have a look." We finished and pushed the dishes and cutlery aside.

The miniature ship was about three feet long, black-hulled, buff-decked and beautifully detailed, down to her red and green running lights and clear range lights at the mastheads.

"It's a honey," said Steve. He pointed at the ship's name, *Centurion,* and said. "Bullard must be planning on more of these. A Roman Centurion was the leader of a hundred men." Another association tickled the back of my mind, but eluded me.

The waiter poured a third round of coffee and we admired Tom's craftsmanship, with an occasional glance at the tow, until Steve said, "They're turning west."

The three of us watched silently as the hunchbacked old tug and the lethal gray torpedo-boat made a slow turn to the right. Tom said, "Well, at least Frank had the grace not to paint 109 on her bow."

"Yeah" I agreed. "Her number's 77. Same as her length. *Hussar*'s length, too." I blew on my coffee. Maybe Ann's death was just a freak accident. Everybody else found it easy enough to accept. Why couldn't I? Or was it, Why wouldn't I?

It was Tom's day to buy breakfast and while Steve and I were waiting outside, up the walk came Frank Bullard and a fellow who looked a lot like the skipper of Frank's plywood warboat. He had the same hatchet face and sharp Adam's apple but was light-skinned, with a blur of beard. Same black brows in a connected line. This guy wore gray sharkskin, though; the skipper usually wore the quasi-military uniform of most professional boat handlers—tan slacks, brass belt buckle, tan shirt with button-down pockets and shoulder straps.

Frank was dressed for the city in light gray suit, white shirt and red tie. He was carrying his coat over one arm and as he came up to us I made an attempt at amiability.

"Tom's model of your ship's a beauty, Frank. Why *Centurion,* though? I'd have expected something taurine, like the PT." I waved toward the westbound boats.

He eyed me, checking to see if I were in earnest.

"It's a tradition of my grandfather's. He was a great admirer of the Romans. All our ships have names like that."

"Oh?"

"Yeah, *Consul, Caesar, Centurion.*" He turned away, then paused and turned back.

"Hey, Wallace, you're the big-shot boat expert. Do you know how a propeller works?"

"There are three theories about how a propeller works. Which one you use depends on what..."

"Nah, nah. A propeller is like the wing of an airplane—it *flies* through the water." He made a sweeping motion with his free arm. "That old tin boat of yours rusted away yet?"

My back was starting to stiffen and my reply had a

little heat, "Frank, my boat is made of Monel. It's an alloy of copper and nickel. Doesn't rust, pit peel or corrode; in many ways, it's stronger than steel."

"Yeah, sure, sure," said Bullard.

He walked up the steps and grabbed the handle of the door. As he opened it Tom came out and I was struck by Bullard's size. He and Tom were pressed pretty close together for a moment, and I saw that Frank was darn near as large as Tom, maybe an inch shorter and an a few inches narrower, but that was all. Taking the box from Tom, Frank and the five-o'clock shadow slid through the doorway.

"Boy," I said as Tom trotted down the stairs and joined us, "Bullard may know how to make pots of money running tankers, but he doesn't know much about how they work. That plywood toy of his is the original throw-away boat. Truest thing ever said about PTs is 'They were expendable.'

I glared at the door of the diner. "You know, Steve, I think I should have quoted him Psalm 50."

Steve gave an emphatic thumbs-down sign. "Hadrian, you'd have looked like a bigger ass than Bullard.' He grinned, "Tough act to follow, I admit, but that would have done it."

"What's this verse?" asked Tom.

"I will accept no bull from your house," Steve replied.

Tom shook his head and laughed. "Mother Sea! How do you guys know this shit?"

Steve said, "I have a photographic memory and a thorough Hebraic education, neither of which I have been able to overcome. What Wallace's excuse is I don't know." His teeth gleamed in a wicked smile.

On that note we parted, Tom to his boat shop, Steve to his office, I to stroll across the footbridge to see if I could find the spot where Ann and Frank had stood at moonrise to toss coins in the water.

IT WAS LOW TIDE and, to my chagrin, there was a very likely-looking pool and it was a good deal closer to the mainland than to the marina; just a dozen paces or so from the point where the bridge left the shore.

I walked back to the parking lot side, slid under the handrail, climbed down the rough-stone seawall and scrunched across the kelp and clams to the edge of the pool. There did seem to be glints and flashes from the bottom of the pool, so I waded in and began to dig around. I came up with a quarter, then a dime. I saw something larger gleaming in a crevice and stretched out…

"Whatcha doin' Hadri-enne? Gropin' the grouper, hah?"

It could only be Connie Maladetta. I thought she was in Brazil or Macao. I thought I'd never see her again.

I glanced up. She was pressed tight against the railing, so the first thing I saw was a flash of scarlet underpants. I looked onward, found her grinning face, totally lost my tenuous balance and crashed into the water.

Connie hopped up and down; she laughed. I saw red, figuratively and also literally as her skirt billowed around her legs. Her long, lovely legs.

"Connie, someday you've really got to grow up."

"Pooh!" she said, dropping the accent, "Look who's talking. Didn't your Mommie teach you not to wade in the water with your shoes on?"

The bottom was rocky and I'd deliberately come out with old sneakers and no socks. I gave her a scowl and floundered forward after the glint.

Whatever it was, it was square and it was wedged into a crevice. I got a thumb and finger on it, and it moved but then slipped back. I pinched again and could now see that I had hold of the stainless steel slide of a computer diskette. Instead of fussing with the stainless steel slide, I used both hands to tug on the plastic outer case and it came free quickly. Which made me lose balance and splash down again.

I looked up. Connie was snorting behind one hand and using the other to control her dress.

The plastic case of the disk had a diagonal scratch on it; probably happened when I yanked it free. Otherwise, it looked okay. Holding it up, I said, "Connie, do you think this would work?"

The appeal to her professionalism calmed her and she answered, "It just might. I once rescued one from a puddle of beer and got it to work. Do you have any distilled water?"

"I've got about a ton of it. That's what steamboats run on."

"Well then, caro, get zee lead out. We clean up this bébé. We make heem talk, hah?" With a toss of black hair she turned and billowed away toward *Hussar*.

ELEVEN

CONNIE WAS RUMMAGING the galley for a suitable shallow pan for rinsing the diskette and I had just set down a gallon jug of distilled water on the counter, when the phone rang.

It was Sergeant Devereaux. "Can you come to Police Headquarters?"

"Right now?" I asked. Connie and I needed to do some catching-up and sorting-out.

"Yes, please, Mr. Wallace. Some new things have turned up since the inquiry and we need to ask you about them."

I sighed, said okay and hung up.

Connie was decanting distilled water into an aluminum pie tin. She set the jug aside and picked up the diskette.

"Connie, is this going to take a while? I have to go downtown." I paused to watch her slide the diskette into the water and begin tilting the pan back and forth. She'd let her hair grow below her shoulders and, turned away as she was, I was strongly reminded of Ann. "Do we need to talk about anything?" I guess I kind of blurted it out, because Connie turned to me, smiling and twinkling, "Caro, don't look so serious. I'm not here to get back in your life. You are very much upset by the death of Ann Bullard, no? You don't have anything for me." She cocked her head and held her elbows. "Sometimes I think even when I was with you, you were with her."

"Connie, it really wasn't like that. It's just that right now..."

She put her hand to my mouth. "Caro, I'm not back to start up again. I'm back because I didn't want to wait in Rio for the Banco do Brazil to make up its mind."

"About your translation program, huh?"

She frowned and nodded. "Yes, yes. It's finished and it works."

"You got the money to test it and get it packaged; all that stuff? Connie, that's great." I meant it. She deserved good things.

Connie draped her arms over my shoulders and kissed me on the nose. "You bet! I got the money and put together a great presentation and demo and..." Abruptly her face fell. "And now I've got to wait, wait, wait." She threw her arms up. "Hadrian, it is hell. I cannot sit still."

"Poor Connie." I was sympathetic, *and* relieved. As soon as she heard from Rio, she'd be off, either to sign a contract or to pitch her program to someone else. "Waiting is tough." And on a deal that would probably make her a millionaire? With her temperament, she had to be just about berserk. I was glad we wouldn't be sharing space. No matter what, it was going to be stormy.

She opened her arms and came to me, but somehow held that subtle millimeter of distance—"this far and no farther." So I held her for a moment, stroking her hair, then pulled away and looked into her eyes.

"Connie, I've got to go. That was Police Headquarters on the phone. You know your way around. Make yourself at home. Use the computer. Take a nap. If you can, wait. We'll have dinner."

We relaxed our embrace and she returned to the pan, the water and the diskette.

"Go, go, caro. I see you later."

TWELVE

HEYOKA IS A CONSERVATIVE society that generally prefers to keep things as they are, but the need to catch up with the times finally hit a couple of years ago and now the city is acrawl with architects, bulldozers, masons, and computer whizzes. Police Headquarters, a part of a new quadrangle going up behind the old Council Hall, has fortunately been completed and is, therefore, out of the main combat zone.

I walked on shining tiles down beige halls tangy with new paint and entered a bright room with about six officers in blue clicking away at computers. In front of me a large uniformed back was hunched over a phone, offering support to a couple of comrades in the field: "Look, both of you just pull up your bra straps and go in there and make the collar. I'm send..." She noticed me and stopped talking long enough to point to a mahogany paneled door to my right.

As I started toward it, the door opened and there was Sergeant Mary Devereaux. She waved me in and followed after.

A large, gray-haired woman in a dark blue dress

with a slightly darker floral pattern, was standing in front of a desk and she gave me her hand. "Good day, Mr. Wallace, I am Inspector Grisonne. Please sit there."

A rule of thumb in Heyoka is if the name is French, the family is old-line and probably has clout. The chair she indicated was comfortable, but I noticed it was artfully angled so that the light from the window fell full on me.

The Inspector moved behind her desk, a richly varnished slab of mahogany with nothing on it except a thin file folder and a pair of gold-rimmed glasses. She said, "Mary, please see if there's fresh coffee and bring..." she glanced at me, one eyebrow up. I nodded. "...some for all of us."

As the door closed, the Inspector sat, picked up the glasses and as she put them on, turned her eyes on me. She must have been slightly far-sighted because the lenses made her brown eyes huge, wise, all-seeing. This was not a lady anyone would find it easy to lie to. Hell, even fibbing would take guts.

"Before Mary comes back," she began, "there's something I thought it would be better to go into privately."

She had my attention.

She pulled the file to herself, opened it and handed me a photocopy of a story of mine called "First Time at Heyoka High." A thinly disguised account of my relationships with Ann and Arianna, I'd written it in college, it had been published in the Heyoka U. literary journal. I had completely forgotten it. Now here it was, an artifact from an ancient time, a kind of Rosetta Stone, encrypting me.

I automatically scanned the first few pages, and I winced in wonder that it had been published. Every noun seemed to have six adjective piled up against it, every verb, three or four adverbs. I felt myself beginning to blush; it seemed so crude and callow.

How had they gotten hold of it? Then I remembered the computer programming class where I'd met Connie. During one of the classes the professor had mentioned that all the documents of the school, right back to its founding were now on computer tapes. He'd had a lot to do with it and was clearly proud of his (leading) roll.

"The point of your story is very nice," I heard the Inspector say.

"How's that?" I replied. The room came back and I glanced out the window at green leaves and clean sunlight, hoping their freshness would cool my heart, hot with embarrassment.

"The fact that the two young people—whom I take to be you and Ann Summerlune—break up because neither really wants sex and can't handle the biological and the social pressures pushing them to it."

"That's the point of the title, all right," I said. "First time anyone at Heyoka High said no."

Her dark face flashed into a grin and she laughed. "Mr. Wallace, you'd be surprised how much talk and how little action there actually is at that age. A lot of kids are scared to death of sex. It means giving up autonomy. Taking up the burden of caring. Ceasing to dream."

"I'm glad it rang true to you."

"The other thing I liked about your story is how your boy used the situation, the fact that his girl had gone on to college before him, to fend off the other one—the..." She paused and then used a Heyoka word," the shemoyga with the hot pants? Was she real?"

"No," I lied," I made her up." I guess back then Arianna had been kind of wild, so skemoyga was apt enough. But hot-pants? Apparently, I'd put more in that story than I remembered.

The Inspector eyed me again for a moment. She seemed to exude amusement and disbelief, but mildly, like a perfume artfully deployed.

"Well, she's a vivid character. Really. The best in the story."

"Thank you," I said.

"I also liked the subtle way you suggested the rivalry of the two girls for the boy."

Did I put that in the story? Or was this canny woman implying that Arianna might have held a jealous motive for murder these many years long.

Inspector Grisonne took the papers from my hand, slipped them into the folder and pushed it to one side. She laced her fingers together.

"Now, Mr. Wallace, in view of that story, and the fact that you had some sort of on-going relationship with her, I have to ask you this: Were you and Mrs. Bullard lovers?"

Instantly, that amazing night on the Atlantic was before me—the dazzle of stars, the high, white moon; the boat becalmed, her sails flopping thunderously from side to side, and only now and then sent ghosting forward from a whiff of wind. Ann had said "Shipmates are forever." Then, in the most matter-of-fact way, she had taken off her clothes and stood for a moment, moonlight become woman. She had reached out for the slack jib sheet, and rode it into the water. Lying back, holding the rope, arms above her head, stretched out, legs opening… "Come on in, Shipmate, the water's fine." A grin, a flick of feet. Glass-clear water embracing her bright body. I entered the water and then her. What was she and what was sea I could not tell.

"Not while she was Mrs. Bullard," I heard myself saying, and I wished I hadn't told that first foolish fib about Arianna.

"I see," said the Inspector. The door swung open and Mary walked in toting a tray with Danish and three steaming mugs.

We mixed, munched and stirred for a few minutes. Then we all settled back and the Inspector got to the main reason I'd been summoned. "Mr. Wallace, do you find it odd that, after being away for months in the one case, and years in the other, Consuela Maladetta and Arianna Lencouvert came back to Heyoka just at the time of Mrs. Bullard's death?"

She gave her coffee one last stir and set the spoon aside with a click.

I felt my temper rising and started to get to my feet. "Hey, Inspector, easy does it. I'm not going to talk about friends of mine from, from the leaves of the tree."

The hefty bosom of the Chief Inspector rose and fell with her sigh. She pulled the file in again, flicked it open, pushed my story to one side. The only thing left in the file was a single sheet of paper, edged all around, oddly enough, with a half-inch-thick band of black.

The Inspector lifted this funereal page and said, "I see you killed a man not too long ago."

"Inspector!" I yelped, and now I was on my feet. "That was done in the name of the Nation. The guy was holding a gun on me and a Heyoka police officer." Here it was again. That business in the Bahamas was supposed to be hush-hush, Never-to-be-Divulged stuff. It happened before this Inspector's watch, so if she had been briefed on it, it must mean they weren't entirely satisfied with the inquest's ruling of accidental death.

The Inspector dropped the page, folded the file and pushed it away. "Yes, yes, I know all that. Sit down, Mr. Wallace."

She took off her glasses, and squared them on the polished wood in front of her. "So, you won't talk about your friends and you don't need to talk about the Bahama sting. Perhaps, then, you can fill us in a little about the boat trip you were on the weekend Mrs. Bullard probably died."

I looked at Sergeant Mary Devereaux whose lovely epicanthic eyes had become perfect ovals.

Grisonne was using perfectly normal interrogation tactics. She had me off balance when I fibbed about Arianna. Now I felt aggrieved, and I was irritated at myself for rising to her baiting.

The grand lady smiled a sere smile and said, "Let's begin with the Friday evening Mr. and Mrs. Bullard said their good-byes on the bridge.

I sat, and I made myself relax all the way back into the chair.

"Take your time, Mr. Wallace. There's plenty of coffee."

THIRTEEN

WHEN I GOT BACK to the marina, there were two notes on *Hussar*'s instrument panel. The one from Arianna read: "Your young friend was just leaving when I arrived. She left you a note. She said something about "reese-cooing thee deesk?" If you're back in time and not otherwise engaged, please meet me for dinner at the Gallery. Eightish? A."

Was it my imagination or was the word "young" emphasized in some way. I slanted the paper away from the light. The downstrokes looked like daggers, driving well below the line of the words, and distinctly longer than those in the other words.

Connie's note began business-like: "The disk is a children's counting-game with a cow and milk pails. Sweet! C." Then came the postscript: "The *madrinha bela* said she was happy to meet me. Hah!"

Connie is rarely subtle (the exclamation point went halfway up the page) and she had chosen a Portuguese word for woman that meant both *regal* and *old*. In English "the winsome matron" might have about the right flavor.

The two notes made me smile, but they also bent my heart a little. God, I could love them both. Come on, Wallace! Grow up.

I sighed and looked at the clock. It was only a little after six, so there was plenty of time to spiff up to eat with Arianna. I looked at the mail—a couple of checks from customers, thank the Lord; a card reminding me to "brush on over" to my dentist, an invitation from a smiling face to become a millionaire.

I walked through my bedroom into my office under the after deck. Connie had left the scratched diskette in the center of my desk. She'd left the computer on, so I slipped the diskette into the slot and a cartoon cow with big eyes and a black and white puzzle-patterned hide was grinning at me. Above her head ran the legend, MILKING THE COW; below was an instruction to pull the cow's tail. There was a little hand floating on the screen which responded to the computer's mouse. I grabbed the cow's tail and gave it a pump. A pail of milk appeared under the cow and a numeral 1 popped up next to it. Another pull, another pail, and the number became 2. Connie was right, it was cute. It brought to mind one of the early exercises we'd had in the programming course at Heyoka U. Connie had been much quicker at it than I. In the time it took me to get a boat chugging along, belching smoke from its stack and throwing a bow wave, Connie had put up an entire city with streaming cars and strolling people, and then wiped out everything with a tornado that roared out of a crackling thunderstorm.

I ejected the diskette and looked at the scratch. It ran diagonally across the indentation for a label. On this particular one, the recessed area ran over the top so that the color of the label would show and let you color-code the diskettes in your file (or stack, in my case).

I turned the diskette over. On the back the indent ran down about a quarter-inch and one corner of it had a tiny triangle of red paper.

I slipped the disk back into the computer and fired up a program called "DeErase" which recovers stuff you accidentally delete. I pushed the Go Ahead button and the screen filled with row after row of squares, paragraph symbols, forward and back slashes, periods, commas, dashes, question marks, and what appeared to be random numbers. It finally stopped and at the end of the last line of gibberish was "Milking the Cow." I wondered if I dared try "DiskMap" and then "DiskEdit" to see if there were partitions beyond the gibberish and find out what was in them. I felt the old familiar urge to just jump in and thrash around. Maybe I'd turn up something. No, it's too long since I did anything like that. I quit and turned off the machine. The clock hadn't advanced much so I decided I could safely have one drink.

Musing over the clinking glass in the pilot house, I supposed the diskette was probably lost by one of the kids on the way to or from school and not something

Ann had dropped off the bridge when Frank came upon her. There was really nothing to connect the diskette to Ann. It was, after all, more likely the lactating cow had been a lab project for the teenagers. Yet... Why was her sock on the wrong foot? And wasn't it odd that no one from the marina had been around asking after a lost diskette. Normally, two or three people a month would stop by to see if I'd found a favorite fishing pole, a handheld GPS, a pair of shoes, a watch, a camera... I gave the ice in my vodka a twirl and took a long swallow, and tossed the rest of the drink overboard. Time for a shower.

The shower compartment has a small porthole which I usually open to keep as much moisture out of the boat as possible, and I could see we were in for a fine night. The high, thin clouds to the west were showing flashes of gold from the low sun and the unruffled waters of the sound had hints of violet.

My gray flannels and blue blazer were still in plastic from the cleaners, there were fresh white shirts in the bedroom drawers. I dressed and passed a brush over my cordovan loafers, I felt well set for a date with Arianna who was always flawlessly turned out. Then I looked in the mirror.

I'd forgotten my tie! I stretched to the hanging locker and yanked the top tie off the rack, a dark blue number with a dozen or so tiny lighthouses that looked like rockets lifting off.

The clock said a little past seven-thirty. Still plenty of time; so I decided to walk toward the Papageno and see if Tom or Steve were at the Three O's Salooon, aka the Three Ohs, or just the Ohs.

The Ohs is a genuine English pub "liberated" from the rubble of London and brought home by a regiment of Heyoka paratroopers. The pub's original name-board—The Yellow Warthog—had been lost in transport, and the new sign with extra "o" had been donated by a painter who evidently had a goodly dram of goodly fere while he worked. It's connected to the Papageno by a breezeway and beyond it at the water's edge, is the Gallery Restaurant, a remodeled octagonal Colonial brick arsenal.

As usual the bar to the right of the entryway of the Ohs was thick with smoke and aroar with yak and laughter, but my cronies weren't in the melee. The room to the left, all green baize and polished mahogany, was as usual more sedate. Two Heyoka men in pinstripes were earnestly debating something over double martinis while their wives held a lively cross-chat, teeth and jewelry flashing in the subdued light.

I didn't find Tom or Steve there either, but I did spot Connie Maladetta in basic black, standing cocked and angular in front of the dart board.

Flick, flick, flick, and she had three very close to the middle. Grinning, she stalked to the target, plucked the darts and turned, arms up in triumph, toward an astonishingly pretty redhead whose face instantly opened in an unguarded flash of adoration and plain, carnal desire.

Connie slapped the darts down in front of the skipper of *Taurus* who was deep in conversation with a gaunt gray-haired lady. The skipper put a hand over the darts without looking at Connie or ceasing to talk, his pronounced Adam's apple bobbing briskly.

Connie spotted me and wove through the tables to take my hands and present both cheeks for a kiss. I complied and was rewarded with her familiar scent of ginger and wild thyme.

"Thanks for straightening out the diskette."

"De nada, caro," she said. "De nada."

"Connie, did you by any chance try to find out if there was anything else on the diskette?" I ran DeErase and came up with a bunch of gobbledygook. I've decided to take it over to a computer whiz I know at Heyoka Underwriters."

"Caro, I had no time. Your lady arrived just as I got it dried and tried."

She dropped my arms, folded hers and gazed at me with a mixture of irony and fondness, "Caro, you don't waste time pining, do you? La Lencouvert is a dish."

For the first time it occurred to me that Arianna might very well look in here if she too were early. The backs of my ears began to heat up.

"Oh, Arianna's an old friend," I said in what I hoped was a casual way.

Connie eyed me, twinkling, not fooled. "Yes," she said, "that I can see. And very good for you, I think."

She took my hand, saying briskly, "Now you come and meet my friend. She is a *genius*."

The roseate genius sat in a cloud of off-white lace and acknowledged me with a thin smile and an uplifted chin. Her name was Louise Harnet and she was obviously in the grip of some strong emotion. Jealousy, perhaps?

The mood of the young genius prevented a convivial flow, but it did let me break away more quickly than I might, had Louise been more congenial.

I did learn that she was, at least in Connie's glowing opinion, the reason the language-translation program was a reality. The Bank of Brazil was ready to buy, the plant in Macao was ready to roll, and they just about had enough money between them and a bank in Hong Kong to finance the project. "Hadri-enne, we're going to be rich!" were Connie's exuberant last words as she hugged the lovely Louise. I broke away with a touch to Louise's long-boned fingers, a peck on Connie's cheek, and "Yay, Congratulations."

There was a mirror at the other end of the room and as I approached it I saw Connie, Louise and the gaunt gray lady with their heads together, talking with great rapidity. The eyes of the hatchet-faced skipper were on me like the barrels of a shotgun till I reached the mirror, turned toward the door and thudded straight into Arianna.

FOURTEEN

WE GRABBED EACH OTHERS' elbows to keep from falling. Arianna was breathing hard; her forehead was sweaty.

"Hey, Ari, easy does it." She was too out of breath to reply, so I steered her toward the door. "You need fresh air."

Outside, I sat her on one of the benches that line the seawall.

Arianna leaned against me and soon had her breath back. "Hadrian, I'm very sorry, but there has been a mix-up with the painters at the lighthouse."

She went on to tell me she and the decorator had planned the eastward facing walls of the rooms to be light and the west facing walls to be a darker shade of the same basic ecru. "I got home from the city and wouldn't you know, the painters had reversed it."

Good old Murphy, I thought, alive and well hic et ubique. But I didn't speak.

Arianna was wearing jeans and a white shirt pulled out and there were paint spatters on both. Her hair was in a pony tail, but lots of strands had come loose. Rivulets of sweat meandered down her neck. I hadn't seen Arianna in such a state since she crossed the line first in the All New England Cross Country Finals and I found her powerfully alluring. I wanted to grab her and kiss her.

Instead I said, "Can't I help?"

She arched back and looked at the sky, "No, the decorator's there and five painters. We're elbow to elbow. It's a madhouse. But we'll get done. We have to. The rugs and furniture come tomorrow." She turned to me with her hands up behind her, corralling her rebellious hair and said with a smile, "Besides, I don't want you to see it till it's done." She rested a couple of fingers on my cheek. "It's sweet of you to offer."

"De nada," I said and immediately wished I hadn't tossed off this reminder of Connie.

Arianna withdrew her hand and her manner became brisk. "Hadrian, there is another thing. I was going to talk to you at dinner, but now...." She drew a breath; looked squarely at me.

"Mrs. Summerlune has asked you and me to decide where Ann is to be buried. She says it's simply too much for her."

It felt too much for me. But, a shipmate must see a shipmate off.

"Of course I'll do it," I said.

Arianna gave me a hug and got to her feet. "All right, then. Meet me tomorrow evening around eight at the oak in North Rock Burial Ground. It shouldn't take long. I have the plat and there are only three choices."

"I'll take the trolley," I said.

"Good. I'll drive out and afterwards I'll show you my home." She brushed the side of my mouth with hers and loped off leaving me with a taste of cinnamon and honey, and the sharp scent of ecru interior wall paint.

FIFTEEN

In Heyoka it's considered the job of the dead to watch over the living, so cemeteries are located on the highest ground in the nation—a thirty-mile bluff overlooking the wide, tidal river of the western boundary.

When I arrived at the oak and the rock, the sun was still above the hills behind a small city on the American side of the river. The river itself was a shimmer of blue cut by the wake of an oil tanker outbound with the ebbing tide. It had been a warm day, but a light breeze was flowing up the bluff carrying a tang of the cool water far below.

The top of the bluff is roughly mown grass, dotted with trees, no others as big as the landmark oak, though. The graves are strung along the bluff by a system I guessed Arianna would explain to me. I, the eagle-eyed boat guru could see no marks. For all I knew I was standing on someone's final slice of earth at that very moment. Not too far away on the right as I stood facing the river, begins what is left of the original forest; it runs on some ten miles or so to the country's eastern boundary.

I walked back to the rock and looked down the road, hoping to see Arianna's car. I had taken the trolley to save a little wear on my ancient Mustang and there had been several cars behind us. One looked like Arianna's but it had a vanity plate, which Arianna's does not. In the event, the cars had all turned right and continued along the main road when the trolley stopped to let me out. Now there was nothing approaching the cemetery except a dark figure wearing a long green coat, combat boots and carrying a briefcase.

There aren't many homeless people or hobos in Heyoka, but whoever it was, the pronounced frontal bulge of the coat said female. Her hair was dark and in bangs.

I looked past her, on down the grade again, beyond a field of bobbing oil pumps, onward to the control tower of the main airport. No car. I turned back to the river.

The hills were swallowing the sun. The water had gone from blue to purple and there was a sprinkle of lights in the town on the other side. The tanker was turning to follow a bend, her red sidelight bright against the black shore.

I started to think about Ann. This lovely rampart would have her soon. She'd be on the black side of the grass. Would that blot out my suspicions? Kill my outrage?

The sky was crimson now, the town in the deep shadow of the hills, a twinkling band of lights; the river gone scarlet. Where was Arianna? There was still good light up here on the bluff, but it wouldn't last much longer.

I turned back toward the road and saw the woman in the raincoat standing by the big old oak.

"Hi," I said, walking toward her and waving a hand. "Say, is there another spot with an oak and a rock around here?" I knew perfectly well there wasn't, but it seemed like a reasonable conversational gambit. Whoever she was, she wasn't Heyoka. Unless she was in uniform, no Heyoka woman would be caught dead in combat boots.

Madame Trenchcoat didn't say a word. She marched straight to me, looked me squarely in the eye, and clouted me with the briefcase.

SIXTEEN

THE BAD THING ABOUT getting knocked out is, when you wake up, you throw up.

"If there's anything good about it, I never found it out," said Alfonso do Floreados. He was leaning against the ancient oak tree, muffled to the mouth in a dark cloak, and casting a single gleaming eye on me. He looked pretty spry for a guy over three-hundred years old.

"Wallace," he said, and he tugged his black beret lower, "I'm not three hundred, I'm one-hundred-thirteen. Why can't you ever get that straight? I died in 1688, the hundredth anniversary of the Armada, which I was in, as you, the greatest living expert on me, know perfectly well."

"Yeah, well, it looks like I was pretty nearly the greatest deadest living expert on you. What happened?"

"Your good lady, Arianna, happened by. Tried to run the Amazon over with her car, bless her. But Mizz Raincoat beat it into the woods. Dear me, *what* a pair of knockers!" The Renaissance genius sighed and stared wistfully into the tree line.

"Hah!" I said, "That's all you know." But the fact that she'd run off (or been run off by Arianna) explained why I was alive and barfing rather than rapidly cooling down to the ambient temperature.

"What do you mean my lady, old man?" I said, retching through another wave of nausea.

"Um," he ummed. "*Her* man would be fairer to say, I suppose. Actually, upon reflection, her is closer to the fact of the matter." The old lecher smiled smugly, then went on: "Speaking of the lady, and I mean this most respectfully, she is no saint. Such a flow of inventive invective, of pungent persiflage, of vicious vituperation! Why, I haven't heard the like since things turned sour that miserable day in the English Channel." A chalky hand appeared from the folds of his cloak and he made the motions of blowing a kiss of appreciation.

"Alf, give it a rest will you? Please?" I was holding my head in my hands to keep it from falling off. I groaned. I gagged. I felt another heave coming.

"Of course, dear boy. By the way, do you, ah, think you're alive?"

For the first time I noticed I was vomiting into a plaid blanket. With my nose practically in the glop. I muttered, "Positive, Alfo. I stink, therefore I am."

The old rat groaned, rolled his eye and, sighing, said, "Ah well, your time will come. Bye and bye we'll sit and chat, you and I. Really no need to rush. All the time in the universe, in fact."

"Where'd this blanket come from?" I asked.

"The trunk of your lady's car. A very gutsy type, by the way, old Hadrian. She had to decide whether to risk moving you and possibly killing you, or going for help, thereby risking the return of the bullet-breasted dragon."

"She has a cell phone," I said.

"Yes she does, but she left it at home to charge up." Alfonso faded till I could see the bark behind him, then solidified and showed me his bright eye again.

"So she put the blanket over me and went?"

"Yes," he said. "Your lady had no way of knowing it, but the demon dame was gone. Had a car waiting on the main road," he pointed a bony finger slantwise through the wood, "out there a little past where it turns east."

"I don't suppose you saw the plate?" I said.

"Why sure," he said.

"I don't suppose you'd tell me what it said?"

"Why not, old boy," he replied. "Oops! Your femme fatale and formidable returns."

Headlights flashed across the bare bole of the oak as Arianna's car slewed to a stop. She left the lights on and leapt out, carrying a bundle that appeared to be another blanket. She was wearing something dark, hair in braids falling forward over her shoulders as she knelt and studied me—sharp lines of concentration between her brows and at the corners of her mouth. She focused on my eyes and then, for some reason, on my ears.

I put a hand up to an ear and felt something wet, warm and sticky. Oh, brother, bleeding from the ears. Not good. I was suddenly afraid, and typically tried to cover it. "Where are my glasses?" I asked.

"Don't try to get up," she said, resting a hand on my shoulder. "They're in the car."

She slipped the plaid blanket off my legs, rolled it up and tossed it beyond the pool of the car's lights. Then she spread the clean blanket over me, tucked it loosely, sat down and eased my head onto her lap.

"Who was that masked woman?" The nausea had let up. Now I was shivering in chill ripples of fear.

"I don't know. All I saw was someone running into the trees. I thought it was a man." She glared toward the woods. "Tell me what happened."

I got the idea Arianna wanted to keep me awake and talking, so I told her what happened. She listened and stroked my hair.

Soon, we heard the wail and warble of an ambulance.

"Where'd you call from?"

"The airport." Her fingers were warm on my forehead, gently pushing my hair back.

"I hope they get here soon. It's been a rough night." I tried to smile, but my mouth felt odd. It tingled as though I'd been to a dentist and the Novocain was starting to wear off. The wail of the ambulance was closer now, and that was good; I seemed to be drifting away.

Arianna looked down. Her eyes were huge and strangely shiny, an effect of the harsh lighting from the headlights of her car, I suppose.

"Tell you one thing, Ari…"

SEVENTEEN

"ONE WEEK LATER, DO Floreados awoke to the realization that those who wished him ill outnumbered those who wished him well by a large margin and he fled across the Channel to Leyden. There he met Margarethe van Rhynne who soon became his sixth wife. Though he always said she drove him berserk, his private diaries prove quite the opposite—he was deeply attached to her and found her a delight. Like many couples, they had one act for public consumption and another when offstage. The eleven years of this marriage were about the most productive of Alfonso's entire long life. During them he and Margarethe successfully floated not only counterfeit coinage but some amazing art fakes as well, several based on discarded studies by Margarethe's cousin, Harmensz. A few of these live on to this day as accepted, authenticated Rembrandts."

I was hearing Arianna's smooth low voice, rippling along. Apparently she was reading from my book, *Do Floreados: Renaissance Cad,* but I didn't see how that could be. I'd only just mailed the pre-pub copy. And why wasn't I on her lap? I could still feel the blanket over me. Where was the ambulance? She paused in her reading and I heard her turn a page.

I opened my eyes. White ceiling, blue walls, Arianna sitting in a chair, head back, eyes closed, the flexible neck of a shaded light arched above her shoulder. The dust jacket of the book in her lap sure looked like the one I'd been shown by my editor—Alfonso in scarlet velvet holding a matching hat afoam with white feathers, and he, the elegant rotter, smirking into a mirror.

I tried to say "Arianna," but one side of my nose seemed to be blocked up and my tongue felt kind of loose, so what came out was a soft and soupy "Aarrph." She heard it though.

Her eyes shot open and her hands clenched the book so tightly I saw her fingernails bend.

"Hi," I whispered. My tongue seemed to work better if I kept the volume down.

Arianna got up slowly and put a hand on one side of my face. Her hand felt very warm. She seemed to be studying my eyes.

"How do you feel?"

"Like glass," I said. Very thin glass."

She bent and put her cheek to mine. That warmth again; heat. almost.

"Arianna, are you all right? You feel very warm. You may have a fever."

She laughed and shook her head, her black hair rippling across her shoulders.

"Hadrian, you are impossible. As you may have noticed, you're the one in the hospital. I'm fine." She reached across the bed and poked a button on a panel of lights and switches.

She was wearing a dark blue dress with small white dots scattered evenly across it and as she leaned over me I had a pleasant perspective. Whatever else might be wrong with me, my eyes were fine.

"Yeah, well, you can pick stuff up in a hospital, you know," I said. "They're full of sick people."

"No need to get grumpy," she said, and picked up my hand.

I started to ask her about the book when a tiny woman in surgical greens appeared. She took me in quickly, eyes widening—startled, I thought. For an instant I thought she was Louise Harnet, but she vanished, and all I could tell about her hair through her translucent cap was it was dark.

I looked at Arianna's hand holding mine. "Ari, are you sure you're all right? I swear I feel a kind of humming in you." For some reason I couldn't talk above a whisper. It felt like there was something in the back of my throat.

She laughed again and it seemed to me her laughter was a touch wild. Her eyes seemed unusually bright.

"Hadrian, I'm fine. Really I am. It's a beautiful day and I'm hunky-dory, all right?"

For the first time I noticed the sunlight. It was flowing from behind me and striking Arianna. Maybe that explained the shine of her eyes.

"What time is it?"

Arianna's smile faded. She looked at her watch. "Just about four-thirty in the afternoon."

"My oh my," I whispered and gave her a grin. "I've nearly slept the day around."

Arianna looked at me steadily for a moment, then took my other hand. She said, "Hadrian it's your birthday."

My heart gave a lunge. "Arianna, you don't mean I've been out for a week!"

"That's right, Mr. Wallace," said a gaunt woman in white, pushing the door back a little as she walked in, "You've been here a week."

The badge over the left pocket of her white smock said Iris Wyndhover, MD. She was light-skinned, about the shade of the freckles on my face. There was a lot of gray in her hair and her face was a net of wrinkles, but her eyes were lively. She might have been sixty, she might have been eighty. She was a lot like Alice Emeu in that respect.

"Give me your hand, young man."

I held up my left hand and she took it and said, "Squeeze, please."

Her fingers were long and looked kind of fragile, so I applied little pressure.

"Oh, come on Mr. Wallace, you can do better than that."

I exerted myself and she said, "Good, that's more like it. Have you always been a southpaw?"

"Yes," I said, wondering that I hadn't crushed her fingers.

"Okay. Now hold your hand palm up and curl your fingers."

She took hold of my arm and hooked her fingers into mine and said, "Pull against me." I did as she said and was shocked to see how easily she pulled my fingers flat.

"God, I don't seem to have any strength at all."

"Oh, that'll come back in no time," she said. "Now, the same thing with your right hand."

When we finished, she looked carefully into each of my eyes and had me follow the glow of a penlight as she looped it around. "How's your vision?"

"Doctor, this is strange, but it seems to be better. I read your name tag when you walked in the door and I'm not wearing my glasses."

"How interesting." She took a yellow pad out of her pocket and made a note on it.

She walked to the end of the bed and pulled the covers off my feet and asked me to wiggle my toes.

"Very good." She moved her pencil toward my feet. "Can you feel this?"

I felt nothing. "No," I said. My heart twitched and I saw Arianna's brows come together and her chest rise as she drew in a slow breath.

"Well, that's good," said the Doctor. "I'm not touching you. How about this?"

I felt a quick stab of the pencil point on each my feet and pulled them away.

"Good," said the doctor. "Well now, we're going to want to run some tests, of course, but I think we can have the feeding tube out. Arianna, I'm sure there are some calls you want to make. Let's leave him to the nurses." Arianna's hand briefly rested on mine and I held onto it:

"The funeral's been, I guess?"

"Yes, three days ago."

"What kind of a day was it?"

"Sunny and cool for this time of year," she said. "but restless. Gusty wind and high feathery clouds, like huge wings."

I liked that. "The angels bore her away," I murmured.

"What?"

"Oh, nothing," I said, but my whispery voice broke. "It reminded me of an old song." I felt my eyes filling and I turned away and asked, "Anything new from the police?"

Arianna dropped my hands. "Mostly they've been trying to find who conked you. I'll fill you in later."

She plucked my book from the chair and walked out.

Immediately, a blimp and a willow entered the room. The blimp wore a tag saying Sally, the willow was Sarah. She was carrying a yellow basin, Sally a white towel. Both were grinning, patently glad to see me awake.

"Happy Birthday, Mr. Wallace, "said Sally.

"And welcome back," added Sarah. She put the yellow basin down beside me. "Now, I'm going to take your feeding tube out. It'll feel a little funny and you may gag."

She reached up to tuck a couple of stray strands of hair behind her ears. "First the tape," she said. "Ready?"

I nodded.

She stripped off the tape and taking my chin in one hand, pulled steadily on the tube with the other. It felt like a zipper was closing inside me while at the same time a snake slid out my nose. But I didn't gag and Sally dropped the towel over the basin so deftly that all I got was a glimpse of a milky plastic coil.

Sarah said, "Doctor says you should sit up."

"All right," I said.

Sally pulled the bed away from the wall and they each took a shoulder and sat me up.

"How do you feel?"

I felt fine.

"Not dizzy?"

"Not at all," I said.

"Great," said Sally. She pushed the bed back against the wall. If you want us, it's the blue button."

"Sarah," I said.

"Yes, Mr. Wallace?" Sally hesitated by the door, but was waved on by Sarah.

"Is there by any chance a Doctor Harnet here, a surgeon, maybe?" Now my throat felt sore and the question came out raspy.

Sarah laughed and said, "Not that I know of and I've been here since the flood. I'll ask around, if you like."

"Thanks," I said and slid lower in the bed.

"Remember now, the *blue* button."

And in doorway was Arianna, smiling, aglow in the sun pouring onto her.

God, I love the green side of the grass.

EIGHTEEN

ON A THURSDAY ABOUT TEN DAYS later, after the neurologists and physical therapists had their way with me, I was let out of the hospital, feeling pretty fit, but still scheduled for more sessions with them and their ingenious methods of torture. Steve Holm and Tom Sorrell met me and drove me to the marina.

It was an unusually fine day for high summer, temperature in the mid seventies, Eskar Island sharp across the sound, a light breeze from the northwest riffling dark streaks on the water.

Steve slid the car smoothly into a parking slot near the ramp and I hopped out and started off.

But they were having none of it. Tom took one elbow and Steve the other and the two of them skimmed me swiftly down the ramp and along the docks to my boats.

The tide was up. *Hussar* looked fresh and bright. So did *Kindred Spirit,* my sailboat. She was dancing lightly on the sparkling water, looking as airborne as I had felt just moments before.

Tom and Steve allowed me to climb the boarding

stairs alone, though I could tell they were poised to grab me if I tottered. I paused at the top of the platform to take things in at a more leisurely pace.

"Wow, you guys did great by the boats!" The docklines of both boats were lying in tight spiral mats next to the cleats, something I thought okay for boat shows, but kind of putting on the dog otherwise. "Better than I would have, in fact."

In the course of a lot of other catching-up and filling-in, I'd been told that Steve and Tom and Manny Arecibo, the manager of the Sheldrake Shipyard, had run *Hussar* out to the Flyaway Island Boat Yard because Sheldrake was full up with fitting engines in *Taurus* and completing two new party fishing boats. I'd figured that meant *Hussar*'s bottom had been cleaned and painted, but now it looked like the decks and topsides had been painted and the mahogany trim varnished, as well. "I was going to let the varnish go this season," I said.

"We had a lot of help," said Steve with a wry grin. "I actually had to *ask* the yard for the bill and when they finally came up with it, it was ridiculously low."

An awful lot of kindness had been dumped on me in the last couple of weeks; this was just one more straw on the stack. Who would have thought those rough old jokers on that tight little island...

"Hey, Hade, you feeling all right?" Steve was looking at me from under a shading hand. "Maybe we'd better get you out of the sun. I don't want to have to deal with PAW Prints again."

That made the three of us laugh. PAW, we had learned, stands for Probable Actuarial Worth, an assessment of what an individual has contributed and is likely to contribute to the nation in a lifetime. It's used in cases of coma to decide when to pull the plug. Steve and Tom happened to be at the hospital the day the Hospital Administrator and the doctors went over my PAW.

Steve walked up the stairs and handed me my keys. "Someday you're going to have to tell me what you did in the Bahamas. The Heyoka Nation was prepared to keep you going for over a year." He was eyeing me keenly. Obviously, Tom had told him nothing.

"Oh, Tom and I and one of the women from the police force went down there and found a missing boat for Heyoka Underwriters Group. Saved 'em a bundle." I turned the key and slid the pilot house door aft. "Hey, how's this for an acronym? Heyoka Underwriters Group: HUG!"

My sally successfully deflected Steve's question and we all laughed and immediately fell into a discussion of acronyms—how they started and how some of them made words, sometimes by design, but mostly by accident.

We were chewing companionably along on this theme when the phone rang. It was Arianna from New York.

"I'm doing fine," I said. "It's nice to hear your voice, though. I miss you reading to me."

There was a pause. Then her voice lowered and she started to say something that I thought was going to end with "come by later and do that," and it set off a painful surge in my heart. There was another minute hesitation, then her normal tone came through and she said (a bit shakily, maybe?) "We'll do that later. There's still a lot of Floreados left."

"Meanwhile," she continued, crisp and steady now, "I can't get out of New York today and wanted to invite you to dinner at the Gallery tomorrow to celebrate your release. My treat," she added. "It'd be nice if Tom and Steve could make it, too."

I conveyed this to Tom and Steve and they signaled grinning assent.

"They're both right here and say yes."

"Good. See you around eight tomorrow," and she hung up.

I was aware that Tom and Steve had sensed a good deal more in the conversation than a simple celebratory invitation, but Tom deftly gave me cover by asking, "Anything we can get you from town?"

"Let me look."

The galley lockers were full of all the right stuff, including two half-gallons of vodka and five pounds of coffee. The minuscule space was squeaky clean. What took polish had been polished, what took paint had been painted. On impulse, I picked up the access panel over the bilge—clean and dry, the silvery metal of the boat's framework and skin showing just that hint of green that marked it a copper-nickel alloy.

"Guys, the old boat's never been so clean."

"Yeah, well, we know about you and bilges, Wallace." Steve adopted a magisterial air and intoned, 'Bilges tell the true story of a boat's maintenance and housekeeping.' He had me, and I laughed. "Knowing that," he went on, "we had to look after the basement of your darling properly."

"Um, I may have trouble keeping this standard; you guys may have done too good a job."

Steve grinned his foxy grin. "It was the least we could do and we wanted to do the least!" Tom hooted, and with a flap of hands, they were gone. I shook my head at this creaky old quip and caught my red-headed, freckle-faced self in the gleaming metal door of the icebox, foolishly grinning.

I went up to the pilot house again to look over the mail stacked against the wheel. A note from my publisher was a pleasant surprise: Orders had been unexpectedly strong and they had decided to double the initial printing. Well, well! "Everyone loves a scoundrel—so long as he's not a next-door neighbor."—a quote from the old monster himself.

I gripped the wheel and looked at the water winking out beyond the channel jetties. I stroked the gleaming mahogany dashboard, "We'll go for a spin soon, old tiger."

I looked astern toward my sailboat, and noticed a tan van pull into the parking lot. Two men began unloading bags and boxes. Weekend supplies for *Taurus,* maybe?

My eyes still hadn't reverted to their normal near-sighted state, which bugged the doctors no end. They knew there had to be swelling somewhere, because the change in my vision must mean a change in the shape of my eyeballs, but no scan or test showed any. The only other oddity they had found were gaps in what they termed my *memoire recherche;* things I'd learned from research. I'd tipped them off to this when I discovered that there were parts of my book I couldn't remember writing.

Well, they could advance their careers by publishing papers in the medical journals, and good luck to them. Meanwhile, my vision was probably the equal of Tom's. For sure, I was able to read the tastefully-tiny lettering on the distant truck with ease: "Hic & Ubique. Here and Everywhere. We Deliver."

I saw Tom turn off for his boat and watched as Steve eased the car away, and it came to me that I was very tired. I looked at my hands gripping the rim of the wheel, squinted out over the bow, looked along the rail to the flag blowing back toward me at the stern. My God, *Hussar* seemed huge! Could I really handle her? I knew I had, but right now it seemed a fantasy.

I decided I'd make a drink and watch sunset from the pilot-house settee. Well, first I'd sit a bit on the worn, comfortable old leather. *Then* I'd make the drink.

NINETEEN

TOM AND STEVE and I were sitting with our drinks in a booth by the southern bank of windows at the Gallery Restaurant. The paintings on the mahogany walls of the old octagonal arsenal were aglow in the sunset, and the room was warm with food and folk, humming with conversation and the clicks and clinks of silverware on china.

I knew those encircling oils—Heyoka's Grande Dames—and I knew the story of the lone man in that ring, the fatal-eyed messenger of French and Indian ruin, Jean Pierre Lencouvert, Arianna's Grandfather-of-many-greats. Normally, with the Gallery in full flood like this, with my friends around me, with me around a martini and anticipating a stunning woman, I'd be aglow too.

This evening, however, my shipmates seemed to have decided I'd not only been relieved of my spectacles but a few of my marbles as well because I had just wondered aloud if the attack on me had something to do with Ann's death. They exchanged glances of the type that says "O, God, here we go again."

Tom's drink was bourbon and in his big hands the tumbler looked like a shot glass. He turned it slowly with the tips of his fingers, then looked up and said, "You know, Hade, anything is possible, but without a description of a real person to go on, the police are stymied. Hell, everyone is stymied." He paused to look at me, then began to rotate the glass again. "What we should do is get back to living. When your memory returns, then we can pick up that thread and see where it leads."

Tom was right. The doctors' opinion was that the initial whack of the briefcase—which I remembered vividly—was only part of the picture. There had to be more. The attacker was so close, for instance, that I must have seen her face clearly; and in time I would remember.

That was the doctor's opinion, but I wasn't so sure. I was scrambled. Just the fact that I now had perfect vision proved something major had moved in my head. Then too, I'd seen Alfonso, three-hundred years dead; even chatted him up.

I hadn't told the doctors that part. What the hell, they'd been insufferably smug as it was. If they'd heard that, they never would have let me out.

I glanced toward the doorway and there was Arianna in a dress of creamy yellow, her hair caught high in the back; flowing down in an ebony waterfall.

As she strode toward us, I thought I heard a hint of

Herr Wagner's bridal march from the piano in the middle of the room and threw a glance that way. Alice Emeu briefly raised a claw from the keyboard and gave a waggle and a leer.

Understated as always, Alice wore an electric green dress with Mandarin collar and a scarlet wig speared with a large yellow feather.

We stood to our feet to greet Arianna and the tune segued into the Marche Militaire. She gave us each a sisterly kiss and we sat. The waiter materialized; Arianna ordered scotch.

"We were just talking about Hadrian's blank on the details of his attacker," said Steve.

Arianna took a sip of her drink and a drop of it hung on her upper lip until she took a breath. "I wish I'd run that broad over!"

This set the three of us grinning and Steve said, "Wow, wouldn't that have been a sight!" We all savored this vision.

Steve touched Arianna's glass with his and said, "Hey, Hadrian's here today because of you, because you took care of him." Tom looked at Arianna and tossed back his thimble of bourbon in agreement.

Tom, Steve and Arianna had become great pals in their mutual concern about me. Now, they often talked as though I were a piece of shared property, like a ski chalet or a horse. Also, they tended to cosset. Steve's move at the marina to get me out of the sun was just one tiny example of their mother-hen attitude. "Look," said Steve, "let's order. I've got to meet someone downtown in an hour and I think Tom's got someone to see also."

Tom nodded. "Man's coming to look at his rowing shell before I put the deck on."

We shared champagne, laughter and seafood and I decided I'd probably get my life back into my own hands eventually. After all, they all had plenty to do in their own. They couldn't drown me in TLC forever. In the meantime, their fussing wasn't all that difficult to take.

After Tom and Steve departed, Arianna and I shared a second pot of coffee and listened to Alice rippling away at Puccini. She slid into *che gelida manina* and I reached over and took Arianna's hand. "Your hand's not cold, but it sounds like Alice is needling with notes again."

Arianna just shrugged and smiled and rolled her eyes.

"She looks like the marquee on the Papageno," I said.

"She should be so subdued," said Arianna. Then she laughed and signaled for the check.

As we walked out, more Puccini came trailing after us. "Now she's playing *nessun dorma*: 'No sleep tonight.' Whatever could she mean by that?"

"I haven't the faintest idea," said Arianna. She took my hand and said, "Here, walk me home. I promised to show you my eyrie tonight."

"So you did," I said, as my heart skipped a beat.

We passed by the diner, its neon bonnet in full fizz. We stepped onto the island via the old and shabby stairs just before the marina ramp, and were on the access road to the lighthouse. "I'm going to have to spend some money on those stairs, but the road is okay."

The macadam slanted uphill through a thin stand of trees and we came into the open on the rock cap of the eastern end of Arkady Island. The island was quite high here, so there had been no reason to make the lighthouse very tall. It was a cone made of the same granite as the seawalls of the marina and was shaped rather like a salt shaker. There were three stories, the upper one a ring of glass. A new roof and deck circled the building.

Arianna took me completely around and we paused for a moment to watch the new beacon on Talon Rock that had replaced the lighthouse. The water was mirror calm and each flash from the rock laid a fiery ribbon on it. My eyes followed the red line to the rock, just awash now at high tide: Ann's body must have gone by out there…

Arianna gave a tug and we were at the front door again. New oak with a fan of lighted panes across the top. I could smell the fresh varnish.

"Do you like it?" she asked.

"It's marvelous."

She leaned toward me and I leaned toward her and we met at the nose. Her eyes had a twinkle that said she was smiling. She put her hands behind my head and tilted it and she put her lips to mine. Her mouth was like warm honey and electricity; and so eager. I pulled myself to her, and in the dark current of the kiss I felt the places where our bodies met go hot.

We may have been that way an instant or an hour. Then on some mysterious female-male signal, we broke.

Arianna's eyes were shining, black. She leaned back in my arms and, looking at me carefully, much as she had that night of the attack, but with a wry wrinkle at one corner of her mouth. She had sensed the ghost of Ann.

"Hadrian, are you really interested in me?"

"Arianna, of course I am."

She stood on tip toe, holding me by the wings of my shirt collar, her eyes straight into mine. "This has been between us since high school, hasn't it?"

"Yes; yes, it has."

At that, she grabbed me by the belt, hauled me across the threshold, and slammed the door.

TWENTY

IT MUST HAVE BEEN ABOUT four in the morning when I awoke. The windows were a gray ring around the room. Arianna's back was against my side, her hair cushioned on my shoulder, a couple of strands brushing my face—apparently what had awakened me. I silently lifted them clear and saw that they weren't pure black. They had sparks of red and gold. I turned the strands this way and that, making the tiny gleams leap and quiver.

Arianna was breathing slowly and with a slight whistle, like a kettle simmering at a distance—an effect, perhaps, of the little gap between her front teeth. So much for the pianistic prophesy of "no sleep" that night. We are both of us, after all, at an age when enough is sufficient.

I lifted my head and saw a glow across the room which had to be a night light in the bathroom, so I eased out of bed and went into it. When I came out I walked over to the seaward side of the room and looked out at the sound.

The water was glassy and gray. A crescent moon

was resting on the eastern horizon. At the Point Disappointment tanker terminal, welding torches made a sparkling constellation that looked like an oil rig slanted way over—a leaning tower of pelf. It was an apt symbol for the former marsh into which Yankee America sank dry oil well after dry oil well during the First World War. At war's end, with the price of oil plunging, they named the place Disappointment, toppled their towers, trucked them away, and cut their losses by selling the land—truth be told, a miserable cattail swamp—back to the Indians.

Away toward Eskar Island, were a pair of high white lights, and under them a red—an outbound tanker.

As I watched the ship creep along against the lights of the towns on the farther shore, another red light moved into my field of vision and I saw it was the PT boat, her numbers very white in the light of the moon. She ambled along for a while, slanting toward the middle of the sound. When she was about two miles out there was a sudden slash of white from her stern and she shot off in the general direction of the ship.

Even from that far away and through the doubled panes of glass I heard the thrum of her engines. She curved a little left and it looked like she was definitely aiming to intercept the tanker…

"Ouch! Hey, lady, easy does it, that's a private part!"

"Not any more," said Arianna. She hugged me from behind, put her chin on my shoulder, "Whatcha up to?"

"Oh, doing what I do best," I said. "Looking out the window." I tried to turn around, but she held me clamped in her arms.

"Take it from me, Whitefella, that's not what you do best."

WHEN I NEXT AWOKE, the room was flooded with light; reflections from the water were rippling on the ceiling. Arianna wasn't in the room, but there was coffee in the air and a few moments later she walked in with two steaming mugs and a red apple on a white tray.

She was wearing a terry-cloth bathrobe and had her hair gathered in the back with a red ribbon. She handed me the tray and dropped the robe on the floor. Lord, Lord, the only thing lovelier than Arianna with clothes is Arianna without.

Demurely lifting her corner of the sheet to her chin, she glided into bed beside me. I settled the tray between us and handed her a mug. With a "thank you, sir," she picked up the apple, bit and handed it to me. I took a bite from the same place and we sat there, underneath the ring of rippling light, sipping coffee and passing the apple back and forth.

The coffee gone, Arianna took a final nibble from the apple. I eyed the core and said, "If we're going to follow the script we should now get into our fig leaves."

She grinned and got up and stood alongside the

bed. Once again the full sight of her was almost painful. "Oh, let's take a shower first," she said.

I slid out on her side to take her in my arms. "Okay, I'm your man."

Her happy laugh echoed from the circle of bright glass. "Hadrian," she said, "I do believe you are."

TWENTY-ONE

IT WAS JUST ABOUT NOON when I arrived at the marina; tide on the flood and a light breeze from the southwest brushing my face as I walked toward *Hussar*. It was more like a day in June than August.

Someone—probably Tom—had rigged the white dacron cover across the boom of my sailboat to preserve the varnished seats and floorboards.

As I hopped up the stairs and into the pilot house, the thought struck me that if I wanted my friends to stop cosseting me, I should take back the routine boat-keeping chores. Inwardly saying "shape up, Wallace," I trotted below and walked aft to my office.

A green light was languidly flashing on the answering machine—one message. I pushed Replay, hoping it would be a routine request that I could ignore for a day because after last night, I wanted a nap.

However, a crisp female voice came on and said, "Mr. Wallace, Mrs. Summerlune would like to say she is so very glad to learn of your recovery and would it be possible for you to visit her today, Friday, between one and four this afternoon? If you can make it, there is no need to return the call. If you can't, however, please let us know." She gave the number and I scribbled it on my desk calendar.

I might have been able to put an assignment from Heyoka Underwriters out of my mind to catch a few winks, but this call from Ann's mother was unsettling. What could she want?

I went to the galley, put coffee on, and idly began to cut the corners off a block of cheddar and eat it with torn-off chunks of French bread.

The Summerlune's house is across the harbor from the Gallery and has a dock with a ramp to a flagstone terrace, so I decided I'd sail. With the wind and tide behind us, it would be easy. Besides, *Kindred Spirit* deserved an outing.

The coffee was done, so I poured three-quarters of a mug and added cold water from the tap. It didn't taste too great, but the caffeine would liven me up.

Kindred Spirit's sails and rudder were stowed in the boat and when I had rigged them and lowered the centerboard halfway, I untied the dock lines and stepped aboard as the wind pushed us away from the float. I yanked the jib sheet, the bow spun clear of *Hussar*'s stern, the water under us chirped as we picked up speed and I headed for the gap between the breakwater and the shore.

We shot through and swayed along toward the light on Talon Rock. If I sailed over the shallows between the rock and the lighthouse, I thought I might see Arianna if she happened to be near a window. Automatically, I raised the centerboard and the rudder, leaving just enough blade down to steer. Ann had thought of this trick on the return leg of a race years ago and won us a silver punch bowl. Somewhere I had a picture of her in her red windbreaker hugging that ornate trophy, her whole expression radiating wicked glee. The race committee had banned the maneuver forthwith and forever.

As we glided over the clams and weed a foot below us in the clear water, I did not spot Arianna at a window of her tower. I wondered if she was up there, clicking away at her keyboard as she said she must, or if she'd gone back to bed. I felt alert, and happy to be out on the water, but my head was light and my eyes itched.

As we cleared the reef, I plunged the rudder back down, lowered the board and began a lazy slalom through the boats moored in the outer reaches of the Heyoka Yacht Club. As usual, the current was stronger here in the deepwater among the boats than at the shoals off the lighthouse. I looked toward the Gallery and picked out the rock ledge where Ann was supposed to have slipped and drowned.

The panel at the inquest had agreed with the theory that Ann's body had been carried by tidal currents across the bar and into the marina through the cut in the breakwater, exactly the reverse of the way *Kindred Spirit* and I had just come. Looking back at the ledge and the shoal and seeing how strong the current was running past the moored boats, it seemed to me far more likely that Ann's body would have been swept into the sound and away to the east, toward Flyaway Island.

I found myself wishing I could be like Steve and Tom and leave it to the police, but Ann and I had happily sailed our youth away out here and I couldn't cross this harbor and not have her come to me. Good thing we had never played in the lighthouse. It might have bruised a beautiful night.

My boat and I skimmed by the tiny island in the middle of the harbor and the Summerlune's house came into view—three stories of weathered brick with chimneys on each end and a blue awning over the terrace. On the seawall at the right-hand corner of the property was the thing I loved most about Ann's place—the clock tower.

It is an ivy-covered brick folly built before the Revolution by a club of amateur astronomers. Its chimes are so melodic and so much a part of maritime Heyoka that it was front page news when they were kept silent during the Second World War. There had been foggy times when Ann and I found our way to the dock by homing in on the shimmering ring of its carillon.

Here was the dock.

I swung right and let the wind push the boat sideways onto it, sails idling free. As I got them down and tied the boat up, the chimes sang their full melody and then tolled twice.

I walked up the ramp, rather expecting to find Mrs. Summerlune outside on such a fine day, but she wasn't; so I walked on past a glass-topped table and a formal square of wicker chairs, toward the front of the house. As I came around the corner the gaunt lady I'd seen at the Three Ohs with Connie and Hatchet Face came stiffly and swiftly down the walk toward a maroon car idling at the curb. She wore a shade of pink that clashed with the car and she looked angry. She slammed the door as she slipped into the passenger seat, and the car was off with a roar and a squeak of tires.

The door of the Summerlune's house gleamed with countless layers of old varnish and polished bronze hardware, just as it always had. It was opened by a husky young woman in a blue uniform who gave me a smile of flawless white and said, "Please go straight back into the sun room, Mr. Wallace. We saw your arrival."

When Ann and I had been dating, the paneling in the hall was dark; paintings lined the walls and three grandfather clocks stood between the doorways, two on the right, one on the left. The clocks and the paintings were still there, but the paneling now was off-white, the moldings buff. A fringed carpet of blue and white ran from me to the sun room. It was aglow in the afternoon light.

Mrs. Summerlune sat on a blue settee and one of the many squares of light cast by the windows exactly framed her feet. Her tiny shoes matched her gray dress and sweater. She looked dreadfully thin and her eyes, bleak, black and dull, reminded me of old Lencouvert's.

I'd been told she had come to the hospital, but I had not actually seen her for many years and I was startled. In my memory she was hale and slender.

I'd seen her having a cup of coffee with Henry at the Papageno; a brisk, silver-haired woman of business. I also remembered her from even earlier times as Ann's mother—dark-haired, energetic, head of the house as well as the family enterprises.

She smiled and her eyes brightened as she gave me her hand. It felt cold and fragile. "Hadrian, it is nice to see you. You look wonderful. You've lost weight and it suits you." I kissed her cheek which was about as chill as her hand and she nodded toward a chair set at right angles to the sofa. "Sit there so you'll be facing the windows and we'll have tea." She pushed an ivory button on the long table behind her. "My eyes are pretty good. Still, more light is better."

I let go of her hand and sat. The young woman who had answered the door appeared and Mrs. Summerlune said, "We're ready for tea, Susan."

"Yes, ma'am."

We gazed at each other for a moment and then she

took up her earlier theme, "You certainly seem to have come through your ordeal well."

I wished I could say the same thing about her. I sensed that she wanted the tea served before she got to the reason she had asked me here. For want of anything else, I asked about the woman who was leaving as I arrived.

"That was Althea Villeneuve. She said she dropped by to see how Susan was doing. Susan came from an agency Althea owns. You do know she owns *Hic & Ubique?* Althea's one of Heyoka's great successes."

"I'm not much in the business line, I'm afraid," I said. Nor, I thought, in the success line either.

"No, of course you're not. You're a writer, an artist. You were that way as a boy and I'm glad to see it bearing fruit for you. Your book about that Renaissance rip is a delight." A twinkle surfaced in her eyes, then sank. "Althea wants to buy my restaurants."

"You mean the Papageno, the Gallery and the Three Ohs; the whole hill?"

"Yes," she said. She looked bleak again.

"Do you want to sell them?"

"I'm not sure. With Ann gone... Well, I don't know. There doesn't seem to be much point anymore." She folded her hands and shifted her feet out of the light as though the warmth disturbed her.

"Isn't there anyone in the family to take them over?" I asked.

"No. Not… Not with Ann dead." She looked directly at me and her eyes were dull again. Words were useless, so I moved next to her and took her hands; they were ice.

Clatter and clinking arose in the hall as Susan carried in a mahogany tray with a white tea service on it. She set the tray on a low wicker table, moved it closer to the settee and left without a word.

The sight of tea seemed to perk Mrs. Summerlune right up; at least I thought it was the tea. But then she laughed aloud and said, "Hadrian, did you see Susan's face when she came in?"

I hadn't, of course, because I'd been turned sideways and away from the door. "No, I didn't."

"I swear when she saw you holding my hands, she almost dropped the tray. I think she thought you we're plighting your troth, or pledging your undying devotion or something equally romantic." There was life in her eyes now and her face had a deeper hue.

She passed me a cup, poured hers and settled back.

I returned to my chair and waited, enjoying the aroma of the black tea, which reminded me of a kind of French cigarette I still occasionally smoke.

Ann's mother took a sip of her tea and said, "I gather your Renaissance cad was something of a student of the Bible."

"Everyone was in those days. It was one of the few printed things around in any numbers. A student once asked Floreados if he read the Bible because he was seeking the truth, and Alfonso replied no, he wasn't looking for truth, he was looking for material."

Once again she laughed and she looked happier and more the way I remembered her. I wondered if I could keep it up.

"Do you know the story of Jepthda?" she asked.

"Sure. The general who sacrificed his daughter to win a war. It's in Judges."

"Do you remember my husband, Gustav? Ann's father?"

"Yes, of course." He was tall, affable, a little remote; painted bright seascapes. He'd given me one.

"You couldn't know it, but the poor man came to believe Ann, too, had been a sacrifice."

"Mrs. Summerlune, I..." But she went on, so I took a good belt of strong tea and listened.

"Do you remember the uprisings in eastern Europe in the late fifties, Hadrian?"

"Sure. The schools were closed for days. The *Ubiques* were stripped bare. My mother thought it was World War Three for sure."

"Exactly. But for Gus it meant that his brother Paul, and his wife and daughter were trapped, and it was just a matter of time before they lost everything."

"Why didn't his brother emigrate when your husband did?" I asked.

Ann's mother gave me a wry smile and said, "Gustav's family goes way back, Hadrian. There was too much to sell quickly and, besides, they both felt the Americans would never let the Soviets in. Oh, they sold some things—paintings, rare books, sculptures—things like that—to give Gustav a good start, but that was it."

"What happened?"

"Paul started to sell things into the underground and have the money deposited in Switzerland. Every so often, Gus would take several of his paintings to a dealer in Basle, pass through Geneva on his way home, open Paul's secret account and bring whatever was there home. Mostly it was money. Marks or Dollars, though once in a while there would be a family memento." She turned to the table behind the settee and picked up a photo in an ornate silver frame. "This, for example" she said, handing it to me, "is a picture of Gus and Paul's sister. She was killed in the war."

I'd noticed the picture before and thought it was of Ann. Now I saw the girl in the picture was holding a tennis racquet partly behind her and what I had taken for a formal dress was Victorian sports chic. The person I saw within the cloud of white linen, though, was Ann.

"Is this still going on?" I asked.

"No, inevitably there was a slip up."

"Oh, God."

"Yes, but it all worked out in a rather odd way. About the time you and Ann were off on that transatlantic trip, we got word that Paul, his wife and daughter were going into a gulag." She looked at me. Perhaps she sensed the effort I was making to remain settled back in my chair.

"That is," she went on, "they would go to Siberia unless a certain official issued them a visa to emigrate."

"I see," I said. "The visa had a price."

"It was astronomical." She lifted her free hand toward the ceiling.

"Were you able to raise it?" I didn't think so. For sure, I'd have heard about any uncle of Ann's who suddenly emigrated.

"Yes, we were. With the help of my father and Frank Bullard."

That sat me up. "Frank Bullard gave you money? Why?"

Instead of answering, she asked. "Hadrian, how is it that you and Ann never married?"

TWENTY-TWO

INSTANTLY, THAT NIGHT in the sea shone in my mind. I stood and went to stare out at the harbor, not sure how much Ann's mother might be able to read in my face. I began to talk at the pane in front of me, but once my voice steadied, I faced Mrs. Summerlune.

"Ann and I did talk things over. We were on the same watch and it was a slow trip. Lots of calms." I heard Ann saying "shipmates are forever," and "Come on in, Shipmate..." They would never leave me. I looked at Mrs. Summerlune.

There was a subtle glow about her and something bright came and went in her eyes. I sensed she had a pretty good idea of what had happened and it made her happy.

"Not to be too long-winded about it," I began, "Ann and I decided we were shipmates, could maybe even be lovers..." There was that brightness in Mrs. Summerlune's eyes again. She knew; and I sensed she was glad about it.

I started to turn to the windows, but faced her instead and said, "One morning after the morning watch had taken over and Ann and I were getting into our bunks, I got an apple from the galley and handed it to her."

"Did she bite?"

"No, she sat with it for a while, looking down and kind of polishing it with a corner of her shirt. At one point she held it up and smiled and looked at me. Then she handed it back."

Ann's mother sighed. Her cup and saucer began to jitter and she set them on the tray. "Hadrian, I'm so glad you tried."

She took my hand and I let her hold it. "Oh, that wasn't quite the end of it," I said. "I planned to propose again in Portugal, Yankee fashion this time: I'd get a ring. We'd have dinner in a small plaza at a table with candles."

"I never heard about that," she said.

"Mrs. Summerlune, it never happened." In embarrassment I withdrew my hand and rushed on. "We lost the wind entirely, motored for two days. We were very late arriving and it was a scramble to get Ann to her plane. It hurt to let her go, but I had agreed to cruise the Ionian with the owners and leave the boat at Corfu. Ann didn't seem very sure of her own feelings. I hoped maybe things would be clearer to both of us by the time I was back home."

"And you came home to find she'd married Frank Bullard." She reached out and took my hand, actually both of them this time. "How terrible for you."

We sat in silence for a moment, then I asked, "Ann didn't know about the financial trouble, did she?" Of course she didn't; she wouldn't have been on the Atlantic with me if she had.

"No, but Frank Bullard was courting Ann at the time. She was so eager to take the trip it was obvious to me she wanted some time away from him. But with Ann back she naturally had to be told about it." She paused and tilted her head. "Frank Bullard may have gotten wind of it beforehand. He's very well connected you know. Anyway, he must have arranged for the money before Ann came back. They were engaged two days after her return and the money was in our account that afternoon."

She eyed me for a moment, but I was too undone for speech. She went on:

"We sent the money, but my husband's brother and family never came out."

"God," I said and walked shakily to look out at the water. It was a bright blur, the anchored boats, smears of bright paint. "What did you do?"

"We dug in. We worked practically around the clock for years and were able to put the businesses back on their feet. The people were wonderful. They obviously knew what had happened, but they never said a word. They just dug in with us; everyone worked without raises or bonuses. Henry at the Papageno?" I nodded to show I knew him. "He worked two years without pay. And he wasn't the only one. I've never seen anything like it.

"Althea doesn't know it, but she's on a hopeless quest. I'm going to give the businesses to the employees."

"Wow!" I said. "What about Frank Bullard?"

Ann's mother paused, put her hand on the teapot, apparently decided it had gone tepid. She made a motion toward the button on the table, but before she reached it, Susan appeared, put a fresh pot down and carried the other one away.

"Sit down, Hadrian, here next to me." She folded her hands and said. "I know you appreciate irony, so listen to this:

"On the day of Ann's third anniversary, we got an envelope in the mail and inside was a key to a post office box in Washington, D.C. In the box were the passport of Gus's brother, his death certificate, his will and the numbers of six bank accounts in Switzerland that Gus never knew existed."

While I absorbed this, Ann's mother, put a fresh cup in my hands, filled and took up hers.

"I guess there was enough in those accounts repay everybody, including Bullard?"

"That's right." She took a sip and went on. "The odd thing is Gus expected Ann and Frank to separate, but it didn't happen and we were left to conclude that the marriage suited her, and perhaps we had wrongly assessed Ann's motives at the time." She looked at me over the rim of her cup. I felt like I was hanging upside down and knives were being run through me. I didn't want to hear these things. Mrs. Summerlune went on, "It was a great relief to poor Gus. Ann was our only child, you know, and he did want to see her happy."

"Do you think she was?"

"Honestly, Hadrian, I think she did marry him out a sense of duty. But I think then she rather grew to like life with Frank. He definitely indulged her, which Gus and I never did."

Ogod. Could Ann really have fooled her mother about something like this? I didn't think so. In the few times Ann and I had met since the marriage, I'd come away with the feeling she was staying with Frank because she had given her word. And I'd also come to believe there was a definite term to whatever private deal she and Bullard had.

Perhaps Mrs. Summerlune had pretended to believe in Ann's contentment to ease her husband's distress. It couldn't be true. If I knew anything, I knew Ann and I knew she was honorable enough to carry through on an unhappy agreement. But I also knew she was sensible enough to refuse total martyrdom.

"He let her be a princess, you mean?" I managed to make it sound like a question rather than a growl. I did not like the way the tide of this talk was running.

"Ann was a sweet child, but not cerebral, you know.

Not like you and me." She gauged me over the cup and I got the wild notion she was reaching out to me in more than a motherly way. She dropped her eyes.

"In any case, before Frank Bullard got that gray monstrosity, he had a very elegant boat, a little ship, really, and he and Ann were never around after Memorial Day—always off to Newport or the Cape, or Nantucket or Maine. Once they took Gus and me to Nova Scotia, and then on to Newfoundland—the Labrador, as they say up there."

I could easily imagine Ann's father sketching happily away as the white yacht ambled along those rockbound shores and craggy capes from one foggy fishing hamlet to another.

"A year ago, just about the time Frank Bullard got the PT boat, my father died and left half his estate to me, the other half to Ann. Shortly after that, Ann changed her will. She told me about it, but I'm virtually certain she didn't tell Frank."

"Why do you say that."

"Because when the will was read, Frank was patently shocked and upset. He left the room the instant the executors were finished. He hasn't spoken to me since."

"I guess the police thought they might have a motive for murder," I said.

"Yes, but they had already found out Frank was definitely on his way to the Far East. Hong Kong, I believe. Or was it Macao? Anyway, they checked it all out again, of course. But you've heard that by now?"

"Oh, I've gathered," I said. "Doesn't mean he couldn't have arranged it. Could he be in a financial bind?"

"I think Ann would have known if he were, and I'd have picked something up from her. She certainly never said he'd asked her for help. Bullseye Shipping is the major broker for all the Heyoka oil that goes anywhere. The company was that way under his father and the grandfather who started it. Bullseye is solid and solvent." It was no trouble for me to imagine that Mrs. Summerlune was aware of the financial health of her son-in-law, both prior to and during the marriage.

I said, "you don't indulge in toys like PT boats if money is tight. The boat itself probably cost several million and it costs several hundred thousand a year to maintain and operate an old wooden crate like that."

Ann's mother looked a little startled at my pejorative characterization of Frank's toy, but she settled back on the sofa and asked, "Do you still think Ann's death more than an accident?"

I wished I could tell her no. Hell, I wished I could tell myself no. But I was stuck with my true feelings and so I said, "Yes. Yes I do. And I think the attack on me had something to do with it."

"Are you going to try to find out?"

"Of course," I said.

That pleased her. I saw fire in her eyes. Dark Heyoka eyes, not like Ann's startling blue.

"Do you need any money?"

"No, I can't do anything formal. As far as I can tell, the police are being thorough, and, honestly, they can't do anything with my hunches—they're too bizarre.

"About all I can do now," I continued, "is look around and think about what I see. Ideas keep popping into my head, but so far the facts are few. It's like...like two banks of a river...they'll support an infinity of bridges." Mrs. Summerlune made a soothing murmur, touched my wrist.

"Ann left you something, Hadrian. Actually two something's." With a sad look and a sigh, she lifted two books from the table behind her.

They were old-fashioned ledgers, bound in gray cloth with leather spines and corners, much scuffed. I opened one. Sepia ink, minuscule script, tiny circles for the periods. On the inside of the front cover, "Brandeis S. Bullard."

TWENTY-THREE

"BRANDEIS IS FRANK'S grandfather," said Ann's mother. "I found the ledgers in the clock tower on one of the counterweights." She gave me a mischievous eye, "You know… Where you and Ann used to leave notes?"

The clock and carillon were driven by a system of buoys and weights that rose and fell with the tide. Ann and I got quite adept at knowing where to leave messages, so they'd be in reach at the right time.

My neck was warm.

"Hadrian, it's all right, she said with another soothing touch on my wrist. "Mothers have to know everything. It's part of the job." She paused a moment, sad-eyed. "It's also part of the job to go through a dead child's things and it occurred to me to look out there in the tower, as well as through her room."

"Is there anything in these?" I held them up.

"Not that I can tell. It's mostly about the daily operations of the business, work on the terminal, ships coming and going, things like that. Two pages were cut from the end of the first book, but it doesn't read like anything is missing."

"Do the police know?"

"Yes. They showed them to Frank. I gather he showed them where a lot more were shelved in a humidity-controlled room in the cellar He had no idea why Ann might have taken them."

I looked in the back of the top volume. Two pages had indeed been neatly cut away, the line was a little wavy, probably done by hand without a ruler. The last entry on the page before the cut ended with a completed paragraph. The first entry in the other began with a new date, June 18, 1919.

I scanned a few lines. "Any idea what 'es. crew' means?"

"No. I noticed that too. If you read on you'll see it again."

I read: Entire es. crew in hospital. Influenza. Must abandon all unless they recover.

"Kind of odd, all right. I flipped a few more pages. The entries stopped in the middle of the book with one dated November 11, 1919. I sighed and put the books aside. "I wonder why he stopped in the middle?"

"He died of the flu, like millions of other people. I've seen estimates as high as twenty million worldwide, half a million in the United States."

I whistled. "Migod, I've been sunk in the 17th Century with crazy Alfonso for so long, I've lost my grip on other times." Getting conked into a coma hadn't helped either.

Mrs. Summerlune smiled and pressed the button on the table behind the settee and stood, holding out her hands to me. I took them and she surprised me by asking, "If you were me, Hadrian, would you sell the restaurants?"

"No," I said, "I'd do just what you plan, give them to the employees."

She cocked her head and gazed at me for a moment before she said, "It's the right thing, isn't it."

On impulse, I bent down and kissed her on the cheek and she lifted one of her hands to the side of my face. Seen from the doorway it must have looked like we were lip to lip, because Susan, coming in to clear away the tea things, gave a gasp, snatched up the tray and scurried out.

Ann's mother broke into a laugh and gave her silver hair a toss as she said, "Hadrian Wallace, you've made my day, my year, and probably my era as well. Susan and the rest will be buzzing forever."

She walked with me to the door of the terrace and as I opened it, the carillon began to chime the hour. Lord, they brought back memories of happier times.

We walked together beyond the blue canopy to the point where the flagstones met the lawn and as I stepped onto the grass she said, "Now remember, if you need money, I'm here."

I tucked the ledgers under my arm and we hugged. "I won't forget." I gave her cheek a brush for the benefit of the maid and headed for the dock. As I pushed the bow of *Kindred Spirit* away from the dock and stepped aboard, I looked back and saw Ann's mother standing in the shade of the blue awning. When I'd tucked the journals into the carryall and had the boat aimed at a gap between the stern of a blue sloop and the bow of a red yawl, I turned to exchange waves with the trim figure in gray and white. Amazing how lively of spirit and firm of body a woman of her age could be. It didn't seem to me she was ready to give up and let go and slip silently into age.

TWENTY-FOUR

WEEKENDS IN HEYOKA are known as The Mindless Muddle, or the Super Shuffle—you leave where you are and go where you haven't been. If you live inland you go to the shore, if you live on an island you go to the mainland, if you live on the mainland you go to an island. The roads are clogged, the ferries awash, the inns jammed. You run into people you haven't seen in years. That's the main point of the exercise.

In this spirit, Arianna relaxed her discipline and dropped work altogether Saturday morning. We opted for breakfast at the Papageno and strolled along hand in hand. There wasn't a cloud in the sky and the barometer had risen during the night. Going to be a perfect day.

The sport-fishing boats were gone from their slips in the marina and there wasn't a fleck on the horizon, so I knew we'd missed the Saturday morning breakfast melee. As we entered, the place seemed absolutely empty, but then we saw Steve and Mary Devereaux sitting close together on one side of the booth near the kitchen door. I shot a look at Arianna, but she just squeezed my hand quickly and waved to them. Mary got up and the ladies hugged and kissed. I gave Steve a look meant to convey, "Nice going, Shipmate." He eluded a reply by exchanging hugs with Arianna.

As we chatted and ate, it gradually came to me that Mary had something to say but wasn't quite sure she should. She'd look at me, then look and Steve and then look away or be suddenly absolutely intent on spreading jam on a piece of toast. Finally, I said, "Hey, Sarge, what's up?"

"We had a report this morning that a shoe turned up on a beach on Flyaway Island."

"One of Ann's?"

"It's her size, Hadrian."

My heart began to thud and I looked out the window at the sound. Be nice if I were that calm.

"When will you have it?"

"In the ordinary course of things, not till Monday." She looked at me, "But if I could get out there today..."

"Done," I said. "I'll fire up *Hussar* and we'll go." It *was* heartening to learn the investigation was going along, at least at some level. "Tide's about half in. It'll be against us but slackening as we go. We can have a late lunch out there, pick up the shoe, and have the tide with us on the way back."

Mary said she had to change her dress for jeans, and Arianna wanted to do the same, so we agreed to meet at the boat in half an hour.

Steve and I stood as they slid out, and then we sat back down to finish the coffee and get the check.

"So," I said, "how long have you and the sergeant been an item?"

Steve got a little pink and said, "Well, we met in the hospital. She used to drop by every day to see how you were doing, you know."

I gazed at my friend for a moment and decided to do something out of character—shut up. His pattern in the past had been much like mine, short, sweet and stormy. The fact that he was a little taciturn, told me that this time it was too serious for idle chat.

I grabbed the check and went to the cash register while Steve set a tip between the empty plates and cups. At the ramp, he veered off to close the hatches on his boat and get his slicker.

I walked up the steps of the boarding platform and went below to check the water level of the boiler and look up the air vents to be sure no birds were nesting there. The three cylinders of the engine are supported by X-shaped trusses and there are lots of pipes and control cables. Depending on my mood, it either looks like an angry spider or a hunchback on stilts.

There were no nests in the air intakes, so I gave the largest cylinder a pat and went to the wheelhouse where I flipped the switch to start the electric draft-fan and pushed the button to fire up the boiler's forward burner. Soon the needle of the smokestack temperature gauge came off its pin and I left to disconnect the sewer, water, electric and phone lines. I had just tossed the last coil onto the pile under the boarding platform when Arianna appeared and I saw Steve lifting Mary off his boat.

In the pilot-house the needles of all the gauges were hovering around the seven o'clock position. I opened the boiler drain valve and looked over the side at the discharge water—clean and steaming a little; perfect.

Steve asked, "How do you want to handle the dock lines? Wind's a little ahead of the beam. Almost east."

"Take off the aft springs and single up everything else. I'll back down against the forward spring to kick the bow out. If that doesn't do it, I'll use the bow thruster." Steve disappeared and Arianna and Mary came aboard and walked aft to sit on the cabin top.

All the gauge needles were around their eight o'clock positions as I centered the steering wheel, made sure no one else was starting out of the marina or coming in, and gave Steve a thumbs up. He let go the bow line and tossed it onto the foredeck, I pulled the cord to give the whistle a toot and put her in reverse. As the strain came on the line leading forward, the bow moved left and the stern moved toward the dock. Steve uncleated thc stern line and handed it to Mary, I put the engine in forward and Steve unhooked the spring line and brought it aboard with him.

Long thin boats like *Hussar* turn very slowly, so I gave the bow thruster a shot of steam, and we were away.

We slid silently along in air tangy from the weed on the breakwaters. Mary and Steve sat together on top of the cabin. Arianna came up to me from behind and put her chin on my shoulder, her arms around my waist. A gull screeched and flapped away as we skinned the approach buoy and turned east. Arianna said in a whisper, "It's so quiet. More like being in a glider than a boat."

It occurred to me that this was the first time Arianna had been out on *Hussar*. Probably a first for Mary, too. I glanced back through the corner windows and saw her, shoulder to shoulder with Steve, watching the wake. I turned my attention to Arianna.

"Steam is silent. My theory is *Hussar* and her sisterships ran rum between Canada and the States during Prohibition. Up north where it's foggy, they could move and the Coast Guard would not be able to hear them over their gas or diesel engines. *Hussar*'s not particularly fast, but she is quiet and she'll do her max in almost any sea condition."

"How fast is max?"

"About seventeen knots," I said.

"How fast are we going now?" she murmured in my ear.

"Depends upon what you mean by 'we,' woman.

Arianna slid her hand between the buttons of my

shirt and onto my heart. "I can tell about you. You tell me about the boat."

"About nine knots."

"Mmm," she said, "you're doing better than that," and she took her hand away and moved to stand next to me. "Flyaway island is four hours away, then. I'll show you the cottage where I wrote my first Pleistocene Panter, as Steve calls them."

I must have raised an eyebrow or given some other twitch, because she laughed and turned her attention to the instrument panel.

"What a lot of dials, and how artfully set—right along the sill of the window. You hardly notice them. I guess the big one's the most important?"

I nodded. "That's the pressure in the boiler. Some guys can run a steam engine with just that one gauge, but Manny Arecibo set this up for *me,* so he made it idiot-proof. All I have to know is the hands of the gauges should be in the same position. Now, at normal cruise, all the gauges are at nine o'clock. At high cruise all the needles are straight up. That's about twelve knots, so twelve o'clock on the gauges is twelve knots through the water, which is handy. Full speed is everything hard right, at three o'clock. Beyond that Manny says it's time for the lifeboats."

Arianna laughed again and said, "What's this orange lever for?"

"That's to lock the safety valve."

Her eyes widened a bit and she said, "My God, when would you ever do that?"

"When you're trying to get away from the revenooers," I said. It's been used, too. You can see the wear on it. The valve itself looks a little like the whistle, but it's on the back of the stack instead of the front."

"How much more speed could you get, doing that?"

"Hell-for-leather with both burners and the blowers at max, she'd probably do twenty. But the paint on the smokestack would catch fire and you'd run out of fuel fast. Steamers are real hogs, guzzle three times as much as a diesel."

She gave me her wry smile and said, "But of course you'd blow up before you ran out?"

"Absolutely," I said.

"My, my." I think I'll sit all the way aft for awhile. Near the lifeboat."

I laughed and said, "I have to stay. We have an autopilot, but there are too many distractions today."

"Oh, I'll probably be reconciled to boating on a bomb in a while," she said. She brushed my cheek with a kiss and I watched her sit down with Mary and Steve, but not before she'd given the safety valve a long look.

TWENTY-FIVE

THREE HOURS LATER the island was a dark blur on the horizon. One more hour, just outside the harbor, we swung south to pass astern of a pack of small sailboats. The light breeze barely lifting their orange, green, blue, purple and yellow spinnakers, they wafted by; seagoing lollipops.

The harbor was virtually empty as we glided in, a couple of sport-fishermen still in their slips at the marina to the left, half a dozen sailboats on moorings in the middle of the bay, and a few people ambling along on bikes and mopeds past the white buildings ranging the shore. On the hill above the town was the Flyaway Hotel, a low, wide building with an enormous bright green roof and deep verandas. They were packed with people and the lawn was dotted with tables, most of which also looked occupied.

We followed the buoys to the commercial pier at the south end of the town. No one was there, but a sign on the managers shack said "Back in an hour," so I left a note to top up *Hussar*'s tanks with kerosene and we set off for the hotel.

The bar was aroar, hazy with smoke, hot and humid

from the crush of yammering people. There were six damp men making drinks, so I was able to get four vodka-tonics without much wait. I eeled my way back through the throng and found my shipmates had surrounded a recently vacated table on the southeast corner of the porch. It was a strategic corner because it overlooked not only the harbor we were in, but the harbor where the ferry landed, and the airstrip too.

"Nice going," I said, and handed the drinks around. "Did you notice *Taurus* is in?"

They hadn't because they had been spotting and snagging the table, but they turned now and gazed down at the gray warboat. There was no one on deck and the companionway hatch was closed. Frank wasn't among any of the brightly clad feasting folk on the two wings of the porch either.

I shrugged and raised my glass. "Cheers," I said, and took a gulp.

A waiter scurried up, grabbed the four corners of the table cloth and clanked off with the used dishes and cutlery swaying in this makeshift sack, while another whipped a fresh white cloth onto the table and swiftly dealt out the plates, glasses and cutlery, took our order and fled.

Steve pointed over my shoulder and said, "Here comes the next swarm of locusts."

The ferry, barely over the horizon, was just a slash of white over a band of black, an open Oreo cookie.

Arianna said, "Probably not. That's the last daylight ferry and when I lived here, almost everyone took it—to get home by dark. Very few arrivals."

It was true. By the time we were having coffee, a horde of people were shambling toward the ferry dock.

We pushed our chairs back and Steve put a thin stack of bills on the check, weighting them with a saucer. We agreed to meet at *Hussar* in an hour. He and Mary headed for the police station; Arianna and I set off to visit the house where her writing career began.

It turned out to be a minuscule bungalow, backed onto the tidal creek where the shoe had been found. Roses climbed to the eaves, a number of yellow and red ones in bloom.

"My God," I said, "it's a cliché." If you lived in a place like this, you'd have to be a writer."

She laughed and said, "In my time it was all shabby, the shingles were curled, and there was a leak—over the kitchen sink, fortunately. I had a kayak then and there was a dock…"

"Arianna Lencouvert? Is it really you?"

This from a wide-shouldered woman in a straw hat, jeans and a plaid shirt at the corner of the cottage.

"Why yes, I am," Arianna said, and, still holding my hand she moved toward the woman.

"I'm Emily Snow and I've read all your books three times."

Arianna introduced me. Emily Snow's eyes were

green with a slight catlike tilt, the teeth in her smile as even as piano keys.

"It's about time for the next book, isn't it? It's been three years since *The Ravens of Dawn*."

Arianna laughed and said, "It's at the printer's now. If you'd like, I'll send you a copy."

"Why, thank you. That's very kind." She gazed at Arianna for a moment. "Do you want to see the dock where I saw the shoe? My, stirred the police up so." Arianna gave me a quick glance. I shook my head, and Emily Snow shifted smoothly to, "I expect you want to see how I've looked after your old place. Come around back. You can go in and look around while I fix tea."

There wasn't much to see. The place had only a bedroom, living room with fireplace, tiny bath and a kitchen not much larger. The windows and floors gleamed. At one end of the mantle was a photograph of a young Emily Snow holding a baby, both beaming. On the other end of the rough-wood ledge a framed photo of a young man in uniform rested on a star-strewn blue ribbon.

Arianna went into the kitchen to lend a hand and I strolled outside again and had a look at the dock, now rotted and collapsed between its pilings. Mary said the shoe snagged its laces on one of the old nails in the planking. My mind saw a tiny boat in her final haven.

Arianna and Emily Snow appeared with trays and

we drank tea at a table under a red and white umbrella. They did most of the talking while I studied the inlet from dock to sea. As the last cookie left the plate and the last sips left the cups, our hostess put a hand on Arianna's, "If you're going back through town, could I ask you to drop something at the Ubiquay?"

"Of course, we'd be glad to."

She went into the house and came out a minute later with a folded slip of pink clipped to a sheet of blue notepaper.

"It's my check and a list of things I need. There's still time for them to bring the stuff over today. They won't deliver on Sunday."

As we came to the corner at the main road and turned for a final wave, I said, "I guess the boy in the photos must have been her son?"

"Yes, he was killed in Korea."

"Makes you really want to *carpe* the *diem,* doesn't it," I said.

Arianna took my arm. She looked at the sky. "If you're going to seize a day this is the sort you want." A sly look entered her eye and she stood on my feet and ensnared me in a kiss and just about rolled me over backwards.

"Hey, woman, easy does it! We've got responsibilities here, messages to deliver, people to meet. We can't go just frisking about the bushes like fauns."

"Oh, pooh. This is a day off, and there are other

things I'd like to seize. There's a nice-looking bush right over there."

I got out from under her feet and broke her hold and started running down the road with her hot after me. The exercise changed the mood and we loped along side by side the few blocks to the edge of town where we switched to a walk.

The *Hic & Ubique* took up the lower floor of a large building on the waterfront. Steve and Mary, I saw, were at the boat and taking in the extra dock lines. My attention on the boat, I heard a rustle behind me and turned, expecting Arianna, and smacked dead into someone coming out of the store in a hurry.

Instinctively, I grabbed whoever it was and then quickly let go when I found I had my arms around Louise Harnet, Connie's genius. Louise had changed her hair style since the Three Ohs Salooon. Then she wore long hair and lace; now a perky bob and pale green pants suit.

"Sorry," I said. "I was watching my boat, not where I was going. That's my boat." I pointed to divert her eyes from my very red face.

"Oh, sure," she said, "Connie's friend. Hi." She bent over to pick up the yellow package of film that had fallen in the collision, "Well, no harm done." A quick side-eyed glance at Arianna who was taking all this in, a murmured, "I've got to get to the airport. See you," and off she sped. Her green outfit had brought to mind the young woman in surgical scrubs I'd glimpsed at the hospital. If this was Louise Harnet now, it was Louise Harnet then too.

Arianna flashed a wicked grin. "As a way of meeting women, Wallace, I wouldn't give you many points for elegance. Full marks for directness, though. And pretty fair aplomb on the recovery, too." She ran into the store before I could reply, so I caught her attention through the window and pointed to the boat.

Aboard, I stuck the fuel bill in the binocular box and gave the whistle lanyard a tug. Arianna came out of the Ubiquay at a trot. I pulled the lanyard for another hoot and she stuck out her tongue and broke into a run.

She leapt aboard, puffing a bit. Put her head into the pilot house for a quick kiss while Steve and Mary tossed the lines on deck. Easing the throttle forward and pressing the lever for the bow-thruster I swung *Hussar* toward the channel. As we swept around the outer buoy and turned west for home, a plane snarled overhead, climbing, its wheels only part way up. As soon as the undercarriage housed, the plane also turned toward the sun. It was a sky blue, V-tailed Bonanza and I wondered who was in it—Louise? Louise and Connie? Watching it vanish into the glare, I remembered the one I'd seen letting down onto Arkady Island the day Tom and I found Ann.

TWENTY-SIX

ONCE WE WERE CLEAR away and settled on course, Mary came in carrying a brown paper sack and took another bag from it. This one was clear plastic and contained a gray walking shoe with diagonal accents of bright, scarlet red.

My heart tightened. Memories of Ann shedding her clothes in mid-Atlantic moonlight years ago merged with the vision of Arianna dropping her robe in bright morning just days ago. Would Arianna be as stirred up at the sight of the shoe as I was? Probably not. Did she sense the claim Ann had on my emotions? Probably yes. Was she jealous?

To hide my emotion and buy a little time to breathe, I flipped the lever to engage the auto pilot and stepped out of the pilot house.

Arianna and Steve were sitting side by side on the foredeck, her hair rippling on the coach roof. They both turned toward me as I said we were on autopilot and to keep a good lookout. Evidently, my face wasn't totally under control, because Arianna's eyes narrowed and her head snapped away as I uttered the word "lookout."

Mary was silent for a couple of moments while I pretended to examine the shoe through the plastic, then asked, "Do you think it's hers?"

"Could well be. Most of her sports gear was colorful." I looked a the sole. It was slightly green—dried slime, I guessed—and had a scatter of tiny gray cones—barnacles a'borning. Otherwise, the sole looked virtually unscuffed. "It would suit what she was wearing." I looked away forward, half my mind caught by Arianna's beautiful black hair—now boiling smoke, now a leaping ferret—and the other half trying to imagine the voyage of this small shoe all the way from Arkady to Flyaway.

We were slicing into a rising chop because the tide was now flooding against a gusty wind; the white-flecked water and the cloud-flecked sky were mirrors of each other.

"Mary, I wonder if there's been enough time for something to drift from Arkady to here."

"Oh? I've heard the current is pretty strong in the sound."

"Sure, it runs over a knot, two knots in some places. But the tide changes every six hours and then the current changes direction—six hours east going out; six hours west coming in, like it is now."

"So the net effect is zero?" she said.

"No, the western end is more nearly closed than it is here at the eastern end, so there's a slow drift to the sea. I paused and tried to picture it, this brave little boat bobbing along day after day, reversing direction as the moon rose and fell.

"Let's see, the distance between Arkady and Flyaway is thirty-six miles. If the net flow to the sea were one knot, it would take thirty-six hours; half a knot would be seventy two hours, and one-quarter knot would be one hundred forty-four hours.

Steve and Arianna entered in the midst of my mental math and he said, "That's six days and Ann's been dead a month." He picked up the shoe in its bag and looked at the sole. "But this doesn't look like a month's worth of growth. More like a week."

Arianna rolled her eyes and said, "You two are just too salty for words," and vanished into the galley. Steve raised an eyebrow at me, I shrugged, and Mary said. "Anyway, I'm going to check it out with the guys at HOTS."

"Hots?" Steve and I both raised eyebrows.

"Heyoka Oceanic Technology Services," said Mary a little stiffly. "They do a lot of work for us."

Steve shrugged and turned his palms up. I grinned and said to Mary, "We live in a jungle of acronyms. Steve and I were on this subject just the other day. We apologize."

Mary sniffed and stomped below to join Arianna who had evidently put her time to good use brewing coffee."

The coffee was passed up, followed by a plate of

sandwiches and everyone's mood went up as the food and coffee went down. Steve was reaching for the last half-sandwich when he stopped and fixed his gaze aft.

"What do you see? I asked."

"Kind of a feather," he answered. "Like spray from waves hitting a rock. Probably a fast boat, throwing a big bow wave."

I gave him the binoculars. The fuel bill sailed down and I snatched it in midair and stuck it in my pocket. I turned on the radar. It went through its warm-up cycle and a bright green dot appeared in the lower left quadrant of the screen, just beyond the five-mile range ring.

"It's the warboat, Bullard's PT," said Steve behind me. "I can see her bridge and the edge of her deck on the rise."

"Can you tell who's driving?"

"No, but he's got the hood of his slicker up; probably taking some spray."

I boosted the burners and blowers, waited a minute as the pressure rose on the main steam gauge, then pushed the throttle to high cruise and glanced aft. A white bubble bloomed where sky and water met. I turned back to switch on the loran and the GPS, catching as I did the long-suffering expressions and "men-will-be-boys" looks exchanged by Arianna and Mary.

Steve stepped to the wheel and we looked at the loran. It showed us doing thirteen knots over the bottom, which was about right, given the favoring tide The

GPS had us at 14. Yes! Love those geographic positional satellites.

The vivid blip that was *Taurus* was now right on the five-mile range-ring. I pushed the throttle all the way to the stops and as the needles leapt from noon to three o'clock, the whistle of the wind rose to a near shriek and the sigh from the funnel became a roar. Now *Hussar* slashed through the waves, the water peeling away from her bow in a slick, dark curl.

The loran soon showed us doing nineteen knots, GPS nineteen and a half; the PT just inside the five-mile ring. We hurtled along alternately looking at the radar and astern. In half an hour *Taurus* was about a mile away on our port beam, raising a great lather as she swatted across the waves.

Steve lifted the binoculars again and said, "Looks like the skipper. You know, Hatchet Face, not the other one—the one with the eternal five o'clock shadow. Are they brothers or something?"

"Cousins, I'd guess. Thick as thieves for sure."

Steve gave a non-committal grunt and lowered the glasses.

For a few moments we careened along side by side, the PT leaping the waves like a demented whale. Soon she was broad on our port bow and I was trying to work out how much faster she was going than we were—about ten knots, I guessed—when with a bang and a screech our safety valve let go.

Instantly *Hussar*'s eagerly-thrusting six-bladed propeller became a quarter-ton, bronze brake. We punched through a few more waves, the dead prop dragging up a terrific burble astern.

Our four coffee mugs crashed to the floor. The valve on the funnel shrieked, squirting boiling water and steam twenty feet in the air. Then we were dead in the water, rolling. Wide-eyed and tight-lipped, Arianna and Mary clutched the arms of the settee.

Oh, brother, how to make an ass of yourself in one easy lesson.

TWENTY-SEVEN

WITH A SIGH, I CUT BACK the blowers and burners. Steve put on a pair of gloves and went on deck to reset the safety valve while I slithered below to watch the sight gauge on the boiler until the feed pump had the water-level up again. Then I slunk back to the wheel and got *Hussar* under way—sedate and silent once again, the proper pace for an old steam crock.

An hour later, the hot disk of the setting sun was two fingers above the hills of Heyoka, the shards of the broken mugs had been tossed overboard and we were sipping fresh coffee from new mugs and snacking on cheese and crackers. The Arkady breakwaters were dead ahead, Hammerclaw Point and Arianna's aerie abeam to starboard. Life was good again.

"Say there, skipper," Mary said through the mist of a mug, "you sure know how to show a girl an exciting time."

I shot a glance at Arianna, wondering what they might have been saying while Steve and I were racing the PT boat, but she was looking demurely at her lighthouse.

"Mary, I can follow that act only with shipwreck or

collision. I'm out of time today, though. We're home." She laughed and so did Arianna. Life was getting better.

As we rounded the sea buoy, the lights came on in the diner and I aimed us at the glowing "o" in Papageno, which centered us in the channel. I pulled the throttle almost all the way back and we whispered into the basin.

Tom was standing at the dock, his hair streaming in the wind which was coming straight from the dock.

"Steve, I'll bend her around with the thruster and bring her in about one foot from the dock, you go ashore with the aft spring line. Mary, you pass the stern line to Tom. I'll pull ahead on the spring and Arianna can pass the bow line to Steve."

They trooped away, got the lines out of the deck boxes and rigged the fenders and, despite wind gusts, the docking went without a hitch.

Steve came aboard and closed the starboard door of the pilot house to shut out the wind. A moment later Mary came up the ladder from below, carrying her purse and the shoe in its plastic bag.

"Hey, wait a minute," said Steve, "I'll go with you."

I also wanted her to wait a minute. The business of acronyms had given me an idea, but Mary would need to pursue it.

"Mary, could I ask a favor?"

"Sure. Why not?" she said.

I picked the fuel bill out of my pocket, wrote on its

blank side and handed it to her. “A license plate I’d like you to check.”

Mary glanced at my scribble and her eyebrows went up: “Y-knot?”

“Mary, it’s probably nothing, but as I was getting off the trolley at the cemetery the night I was clobbered, a car went by and—well, I just recalled that it had a vanity plate and I think that was it.”

I couldn’t very well say what I’d actually recalled were Alfonso’s last words that night: “Why not?” Till now I’d taken them as a casual affirmative, in the sense Mary had used them just a moment ago. But maybe he’d actually been telling me something.

She turned to Steve and said, “Probably going to be a long night.” She was obviously letting him off the hook if he wanted to change his mind, but he gave her a fond smile, saying, “Wouldn’t be the first time,” and off they went.

Tom and Arianna were on the dock coiling the lines and casting quizzical glances at me. Done, they came aboard and Tom asked. “What’s up, Hade?”

“Oh, something occurred to me. It’s kind of wild, so I’m not going to talk about it just yet. I’ve made enough of an idiot of myself today as it is.” I told Tom about running the boat so hard it blew a gasket. “*Hussar*’s too old to be pushed that hard. I know better.”

Tom didn’t think it was all that egregious and

looked knowingly at Arianna. “Do you get the idea, he’s trying to change the subject?”

“You betcha,” she said, and grabbing my arm she turned to Tom. “This calls for torture.”

Tom beamed and rumbled, “Right you are, first the gauntlet—Happy Hour at the Three Ohs…”

“And then,” crooned Arianna, “The rack—Saturday Night Chili at the Papageno.” Chef Henry begins his Saturday Night Special chili early each Monday morning. It grumbles and burps all week in a black-iron cauldron on the back of the range, to be served Saturday evenings by the maestro himself, wearing a welding helmet and asbestos gloves.

“I’ll talk, I’ll talk,” I said on my knees.

“Sweetie,” said Arianna, touching a finger to the tip of my nose, “you will *sing*.”

TWENTY-EIGHT

SUNDAY MORNING I AWOKE with a sore stomach and a tangled mind. The room was awash with sunlight, the circle of panes showing blue sky without cloud. As Arianna opened her eyes and raised a hand to push her hair back, I said, "I had a dream and it's given me another idea."

She sat up sleepily and her hands did something behind her head that instantly produced a long black ponytail. I can tie a bowline with one hand, but I don't think I could ever chivvy a thousand strands of hair into a neat fall working backwards and blind. "I'm not sure you need any more ideas, but I'll bite. What did you dream?"

"There was this old walrus on a rock in the middle of a pink sea. The waves were washing in and out, surging up to his flippers on the inflow and then falling away, exposing more rocks below. The old guy gauges the rhythm and leaps happily into an oncoming wave, but it snaps away and he smacks onto the rocks. For a moment he's vertical, tail waving around, then he flops over. His whiskers are bent, his head is gashed and he has this baffled, hurt expression: His old pal, the warm pink sea, has betrayed him and he can't understand why."

Arianna gave a whisper of a laugh. "Considering that your boat kind of let you down yesterday and that both you and Ann have been conked one way or another, it's not surprising. But a *pink* sea?"

"That's what gave me the idea," I said.

"Oh?"

"Yep, there's been pink floating around since the very beginning and lately there's been a lot more."

"Hadrian, what can you mean?"

"Look, there are those pink Common Wealth checks that keep cropping up, and then there was the pink dress of Althea Villeneuve the other day."

"Hadrian, that's scarcely a sea of pink," she said with her nursely look, a mix of bemusement and exasperation.

"I suppose," I grumped.

She came around to my side of the bed and looked closely at my eyes. "Hmm. It sounds like this is going to take some time. I'll make coffee and we'll talk."

Arianna headed for the stairs and I headed for the shower.

As I WAS STEPPING INTO my shoes, the phone rang and when I got to the kitchen Arianna was on with her agent, Eileen Dolcevita. It seemed to be about script changes for the movie of her first novel. "Eileen, if they didn't want to use any of the story I wrote, why in the Mother Sea did they buy the book?"

The coffee was ready, so I filled a foam cup, pantomimed carrying a heavy bundle in both arms, gave her a quick kiss, and went to get the Sunday papers.

The lounge/reading room adjacent the Papageno was abuzz with voices and the swish of turning pages as a dozen people commented on the wit and wisdom of the funnies. A waiter was pouring a bucket of fresh coffee into the urn. Finished, he clapped the cover over the steam, dumped the overflowing bowls of coins and bills into a canvas tote and trotted off between the piles of *New York Times, Boston Globe* and *Heyoka Ear* stacked against the wall of the passageway to the diner.

Frank Bullard was sitting alone at the round table by the main window and he waved me over.

I tossed money into one of the bowls, drew a cup of coffee, and sat down across the table from him.

His long-sleeved shirt was rolled up over meaty forearms dense with curly hair. The shirt had wide green stripes, possibly to suggest money. His coffee mug had printed rings on the shipping page of the Globe and he made a few more as he idly turned the cup with thick fingers and appraised me.

"Congratulations on your resurrection, Wallace. Must be kind of humbling to get the shit kicked out of you by a woman, huh?"

For a big man, Frank Bullard, you have a small

voice. Feminine. Like the mid-range of a flute. If you could carry a tune, you'd be one hell of a mezzo; but I didn't think Frank Bullard, widower, would take kindly to the comparison, so instead I said, "Bullard, it was damn near fatal, but I'm too happy to be alive to worry about a little humiliation." I took a sip of my coffee. Too hot.

"Maybe you picked up a little common sense to boot." He was eyeing me closely, not with any evident concern for my well-being, more as though he were seeing me for the first time as someone having substance—and being a little surprised by it.

Into the pause I said, "I saw your boat at the yard on Flyaway Island yesterday. Something happen at Sheldrake?"

"The boat's not fast enough. By contract the boat's supposed to go 40 knots and the best they've been able to show me is 37. You know that kid, Manny Arecibo?

"Yes, I've known Manny a long time. He's about the same age as my boy."

"Yeah? Well, Señor Arecibo came up with this idea of separating the engines and transmissions and mounting the transmissions lower in the hull—to get the shafts more nearly horizontal."

I nodded. "That would increase the horizontal thrust all right."

"Yeah, but it turned out Sheldrake couldn't do the work in time for the regatta we have to make. So they made a deal with Flyaway and Flyaway made the changes. Did 'em pronto, too. I may never go back to Sheldrake. I'm always afraid something's going to fall on me from that brute ugly crane."

I allowed myself to show him a smile. "I know what you mean. At Sheldrake, I'm always looking up too. Was yesterday a trial run?" If so, they hadn't made the speed.

"No. We agreed to finals on a calm day and half tanks." He turned and looked out the window at the cloudless sky and the unruffled water. "We agreed to do it today. Want to come along?"

I didn't want to go anywhere near that monster. Bullard's boat had something to do with Ann's death. I just knew it. I forced a smile, "It's tempting, but I've got a lady waiting for the Sunday papers. Besides, I don't think your skipper wants me around."

"You got that right. Harnet comes from a family of watermen and shipmasters." He paused and considered me from under lowered brows. His chunky face somber. "The Harnets consider you an amateur, a guy who plays around with little toy boats and doesn't know shit about real men's boats."

I was going to throw my coffee, mug and all, and follow it across the table and shove Frank Bullard right through the window. But I saw he was ready for me and realized that's what he wanted. He could sue me for assault and tie me up in court proceedings forever.

I downed my coffee, smacked the empty mug on his

Shipping News, thereby adding another wet ring, and rose, saying, "I'm shattered, Bullard. Shattered." I turned my back to him, skimmed three papers off the piles and left, trying to be steady under an overload of adrenaline and a growing exultation in my heart. Unwittingly, Frank Bullard had given me the connection between his ship drivers and Lacy Louise. Hatchet Face, Blur Beard and the Genius: They were all Harnets. They were family.

TWENTY-NINE

STEVE'S BOAT WAS NOT in the marina, Tom's was closed up, and there was only the answering machine at Mary's, so I left a message.

Arianna and I spent most of the rest of the day in the shade of the porch, reading papers, watching *Taurus* snarl back and forth between two orange buoys anchored a mile apart, and wrangling about my emergent theory that Louise Harnet, the computer whiz, was printing phony Heyoka checks, cashing them, and sending the money offshore via Frank Bullard's PT boat and tankers captained by her cousins or brothers, or whatever relation they were.

Arianna thought there wouldn't be enough money involved to make it worthwhile for Bullard, given the number of people who were apparently in on it. I said money was relative and then I unwisely drew an analogy with the problem she was having with the movie moguls by adding, "If the money involved were a quarter of what it is, you'd probably tell them to take a hike. As it is, there's enough there to make you want to keep it, even though they're playing fast and loose with your story."

In a flash, most of the *New York Sunday Times* landed on my head and I received a fiery oral essay in which the phrases "insensitive dolt," and "typical male" figured rather more often than I felt strictly necessary.

Being Heyoka, I should have known better than to say what I had. As a nation, Heyoka has only one thing on its mind-its children. Here oil and money mean one thing—healthy kids. The Heyoka words for oil and money are, literally, *earth-milk* and *iron-food*. Neither is a subject for casual banter or flip comment.

I managed to redeem myself, though, when she paused to take breath for her peroration by quickly interjecting, "Arianna, easy does it! I understand. You're trying to decide whether to sacrifice your child of paper and ink for your children of bone and blood. It's a bitch. I understand. Truly I do, and I'm sorry. I really am an oaf. An ass. A Goth even."

She relaxed then and laughed, throwing her head back and looking straight into my eyes, hers still fiercely glowing.

"Wallace," she said, "There's hope for you yet. It is a lot of money and I've pretty well decided they can do what they want with the book. I've made more than one book and right now I'm making another. What I can't make is more kids." This thought triggered another and her eyes became glistening slits. She wrapped herself around me and whispered in my ear: "But I can go through the motions, you oaf. Come with me."

THIRTY

MONDAY OPENED IN blue and gold, a reprise of the day before. Steve phoned to say they had gotten in late and Mary had left early, but she had the message and would start a background search on Louise Harnet et sibs. Arianna headed for her keyboard and I decided it was time for me to make a tour of the yacht brokers and boat yards, to show them I was alive and capable of working for a living. The insurance underwriters I'd handle by phone and fax.

I worked my way south along the coast and arrived in Sheldrake at lunchtime to find Manny Arecibo sitting on a scaffold in the shade of the fully lowered crane. He was munching on a foot-long hero sandwich that was oozing red sauce and steam. Next to him on the gouged and battered plank sat his yellow helmet, a brown bag and a blue paper cup, also steaming.

There were no boats on the concrete apron where a black, greasy cable looped back and forth across the full length of the outside work area; a six-foot wooden spool stood empty near the control hut at the base of the crane. Erect, the crane dominated the shipyard and indeed the town; lowered, its main boom hung over the water to the edge of the main channel.

Pointing at the downed boom, I said, "Afternoon, Manuel. What happened—the old pterodactyl die on you?"

"Hey, Hadrian! Nah, she didn't die—this bird'll probably last a million years, just like the real ones. The cable was due for changing and we decided to do it before we haul Mr. Bullard's boat."

I scanned the marina but didn't see the PT. "Where is she?'

"At Harbor Point Marina. Her skipper's got a condo there."

I shaded my eyes and peered toward the entrance of the harbor. Surrounded by close-packed yachts, the gray war-boat stood like an atoll amid surf.

"How'd the trials go yesterday?"

"Great! The old barge hit 41 consistently. Mr. Bullard is so happy he's got the boat here for a complete bottom job. Gonna' cost him about twenty thou." Manny took two satisfied chomps of his sandwich. Tomato sauce ran from the corners of his mouth and he grinned as he wiped it away with his sleeve.

I said, "From what I hear, you ought to get a bonus."

"Yeah, well, to quote John Wayne, 'That'll be tha' day, Pilgrim.'" He grinned again, brown eyes sparkling, and finished his sandwich with a heroic bite. He tossed its brown bag into a trash drum, picked up his yellow helmet and turned to me, “So, what brings you down here?”

“I’m making a tour of the brokers to let ’em know I’m ready for business. Also, I wanted to ask you something. I meant to get to it during one of your visits at the hospital, but we always seemed to get onto other subjects.”

A bell rang, ending lunchtime and Manny looked at the supine crane, so I hurried on. “A year ago, when I was here and we were talking about the PT…how fast she might go, etcetera…you showed me her props…”

“I remember. What’s the question? I’ve got to get this crane up and then climb it to see the cable runs fair in the sheaves.”

“Did anyone hassle you about talking with me?”

“You bet! Bullard’s skipper wanted to know what we’d been talking about and the boss hauled me in and raked me over real fine.” His grin was rueful at the memory, but it changed into a merry laugh when he said, “But now that the boat’s going like a bat because of me, I’m pure gold.” He grinned. “Got to go now, Hade.” He jammed his hard-hat on and strode away, a happy young man on top of his world.

I left the yard and spent a little over an hour chatting up the six brokers in town, two of whom seemed genuinely happy to see me alive, the others… Well, two out of six ain’t bad.

Walking back to my car, I saw the crane rise again

to dominate the skyline of Sheldrake, U.S.A., and watched Manny climb its iron spine. He paused to peer closely into the uppermost pulleys, then he straightened and looked beyond the harbor. The sound would be visible from the tip of the crane, its waters dazzling from the afternoon sun. He took off his helmet and raised it—looking for an instant like the great icon of liberty. His gesture expressed exuberance and happiness—perfect for a young man literally on top of his world.

THIRTY-ONE

"LOUISE HARNET WORKS IN THE Department of the Common Wealth. She's a Supervisor in the Bureau of Demography & Vital Statistics. They issue the stipend checks."

Mary and I were sitting at the round table where I'd been ready to push Frank Bullard through the window Sunday morning. It was now the middle of the afternoon Wednesday; Mary and I had the place to ourselves. She looked crisp and poised in her plain clothes—light gray culottes, blue shirt, a pearl on a gold chain.

"Anything else?"

She picked a pale green file card from a pile alongside her coffee mug.

"Louise's brother, Mark, is the skipper of *Taurus*, as you guessed. There is also a half-brother, John. He's one of Bullseye's tanker captains."

"That'd be old Blur Face," I said.

Mary grinned and shook her head, said "You guys," and then went on. "Anyway, till you put it together, no one knew he was connected to Louise."

She held the card out, squinting a little, and I wondered if she wore glasses in private. "Everybody had such a secure alibi in Mrs. Bull—Ann's—immediate circle. Making this Harnet connection would have taken a while." She focused on the card again.

"Louise Harnet graduated summa cum from Middleton University and came to the department one year after that."

"Good Lord," I said. "That's my grad school! We're old grads together. That is, we're together twenty years apart. Er, that is..." I paused, pondering my scrambled syntax.

Mary smiled and said, "I can't parse it either, Hadrian, but I think I get the drift."

"What was she doing between school and the department?"

"We don't know yet. She majored in mathematics with minors in statistical analysis and computer science. She came into the department when the shift to computers began; about two years ago."

"Obviously, she's a natural for the job."

Mary held the card to her lips thoughtfully. "Well sure, but, you know, I miss the old days when it was called the Bureau of Three Lists." She stared past me, her eyes unfocused. "It was just a room full of old ladies, battered desks, and bulging file-cabinets."

I raised an eyebrow and took a sip of my coffee. Mary went on.

"It was dim. There were maybe six light bulbs in green porcelain shades hanging over these unbelievably cluttered desks. I don't think any of the bulbs was over forty watts. And in there was this bunch of old biddies, yakking, smoking, and moving sheets of paper around from one stack to another. It was incredible." A fond smile flickered across her face and her eyes glowed. Her gaze came back into focus and she said, "Now it's air-conditioned, brightly lit and only six people work there, Louise and five computer operators."

"How come it was called Three Lists?" I'd never heard this story. Might be good stuff for Steve.

"It's from the real old days—before paper and the colonial invasion. The record of who was living, who was dead and who was sick or otherwise in need of care, was kept by memory. The women who kept track called themselves the Daughters of the Three Domains.

"When I was a kid, the living were in the filing cabinets on the east side of the room, the dead on the west, and the people in hospital or on stipend—which is where most of the action is—their names were on the pieces of paper which the ladies passed around and put on this pile or that, depending."

"How many of these women were there?" I asked.

"Oh, about a dozen."

"Were they related?"

"I doubt it. Obviously, the main qualifications would be a photographic memory and instant recall, and those abilities crop up at random. Why?"

I grinned. "Seven sisters who kept the records on tape, which they snipped and passed around or laid away might have been interesting."

"Aren't you mixing up the Fates and the Pleiades?"

"Migod, I am." I laughed. "I'd never have made it in Three Lists, would I?"

"Nope. Besides, the Heyoka powers-that-be consider men too flighty to handle steady work." She laughed and raised her coffee.

"I'll drink to that," I said, raising my mug. Connie Maladetta's pet name for me had been *borboleta*—butterfly.

We were still chuckling when Steve entered and thereby walked into a smiling welcome from a merry lady.

He drew a mug of coffee from the urn, moved Mary's purse over one chair so he could sit next to her and give her hand a squeeze. "Hadrian, didn't you say that the Villeneuve woman had made an offer for the Summerlune businesses?"

"That's what I heard. Why?"

"Well, the word downtown has it the other way around. Summerlune is offering to buy up Villeneuve—lock, stock and barrel." He grinned and tilted the chair off it legs. *"Hic et Ubique,"* he said with satisfaction and a laugh. "Literally buying her out, *Here and Everywhere*. It's rich."

"More grist for your column Steve?" I said. Evidently, I'd been right. Elizabeth Summerlune wasn't burned out by any means.

"Could be. It's going to be a while before I top 'Soul Foods: Corn Chowder vs. Chicken Soup,' but I'll keep trying."

He leaned back a little more to teeter on the balance point. "So, what's got your heads so close together?"

"Hadrian thinks Louise Harnet is counterfeiting stipend checks and Althea Villeneuve is making it look like they were cashed in her stores."

I added, "The money is put in bags and delivered to *Taurus* by Ubiquay trucks in broad daylight. I've seen it twice myself.

"Then, I continued, "they run the bags of money out to Bullard's tankers in the PT boat. It could be going to the Caribbean. Aruba, say. Anywhere a tanker stops. More than likely it ends up in Switzerland. Or better yet, Hong Kong. That's where Bullard was headed, and Macao, where Connie's program is being packaged is just across the bay."

Steve looked dubious. "Kind of a crazy thing for Frank Bullard to be involved in, isn't it. How much money can there be, after all? And there'd be a lot of people involved. Just cashing the checks, for example..."

"That was Arianna's objection," I said. "But, you

know, the checks wouldn't actually have to be presented in the stores. Althea Villeneuve *owns* the stores. She could just use copies of rubber stamps from different stores to mark the checks "for deposit only," and skim the equivalent amount of cash from her stores' receipts. She'd have suitcases of unmarked currency."

"Whoa! Hold on!" cried Steve, and the front legs of his chair banged on the floor. He shook his head as though he were trying to get water out of his ears. "Has it occurred to either of you that this is awfully speculative? Is there a fact anywhere around?"

Mary coolly picked up another green card, her lips a thin line. "Louise Harnet's brothers are connected to Frank Bullard. That's two or three facts, depending on how you count. Several years ago, Hadrian figured out another strange case…"

Steve looked at me, "Ah, yes, the life-extending item on the PAW print. The Bahamian caper." I looked modestly away, but I could tell the point had penetrated some distance into his skepticism.

Mary continued, "Also, there is this item. It's small, but suggestive." She looked at the card, "There are one-hundred and fifty-six Heyoka vanity plates with 'Why-not,' 'Y-knot,' 'Wye-knot,' and other variations. One of the Y-knots belongs to Captain John Harnet."

Mary snapped the card onto the table and shot a glance at Steve who looked dented, but still dubious.

"Also, the diskette Hadrian found? The one with the counting cow?"

"I remember," Steve said.

"About all Hadrian's guru could find out was that there had been another program there but he didn't have the equipment to go further, so he passed it on to HOTS and they found it had a program to generate sequential numbers. It does suggest currency or checks."

"Umm." Steve maintained his dubiety.

I couldn't blame him. Even to me, my edifice often looked like a tower of Jello.

"Actually," I said, "That silly game is the main thing that got me going down this road."

"How's that, Steve asked?"

"You remember the day we were talking about acronyms? Last Saturday on the boat when we were kidding around about HOTS? Well, I had a flash—COW makes an acronym for Common Wealth. Milking the COW is literally what's going on. They're pumping money out of the great Heyoka cash cow. And man, someone's got a sardonic sense of humor, to give it that title."

The legs of Steve's chair smacked the floor again. "Lot of lightning leaps there, partner." He considered. "Look, there must be an awful lot of checks..."

"There are a lot of checks all right," Mary interrupted and flipped over another card. "About forty thousand a month, and they're written each business day, so about two thousand go out every day. They're printed and inserted in envelopes and packed in boxes of two hundred—all by machine. Ten boxes. Makes a stack about two feet high." She held the card horizontally about that distance above the table.

"At the end of the day one of the staff of the Common Wealth bureau loads the boxes in her car and takes them to the post office. Sometimes it's Louise."

Steve leaned back in thought and his chair legs came off the floor again. "All right. It could be done. But, geez, how much could she steal?"

Mary looked at a card. "The average check is five hundred and thirty-seven dollars. If she wrote and pocketed only two a day, that's over a quarter-million a year."

"It's probably the way Connie got her 'financing' for the translation program," I said.

Steve rocked his chair "Let's see, one check in a thousand. Very small percentage. With a new system being installed and the consequent confusion and upheaval anything like that causes..."

Slanted in his chair like a human ramp, he lifted his coffee mug off his belt buckle and peered at me. "Weird, but Louise *is* in a position to do it. There *is* a connection to Bullard—or at least Bullard's boats—via her brothers. And, God knows, Connie Maladetta's got enough moxie to go for something like that." He broke off with a wry smile.

Without doubt, he was thinking of the storms and squalls between Connie and me—eruptions he characterized as "Connie and Hade giving each other lessons in temperament."

"You know," he went on, "if Connie and Louise financed the publication and marketing of their program themselves, instead of borrowing, they'd make a ton more."

"Hey!" I cried, "A motive."

"Still, you've got no real evidence. With computer-fraud the evidence tends to be tenuous. That disk could have come from anywhere."

"We're checking on that," said Mary. "Meanwhile, the bank microfilms all checks and the department is putting the ladies of Three Lists back in their element, rooting through mountains of paper."

"Still, Hadrian's disk is your only hard clue," Steve said.

"Yes it is. But we now think it's the tip of the iceberg."

"How come you didn't get onto this before?"

"Hadrian was the only one who had seen anything, the disk, the PT boat heading for the tanker. The main thing, though, is there was nothing to connect Louise to Frank Bullard. That would have put her into our net of people to question in connection with Ann's death."

"Do you think that might be why Hadrian was attacked?"

"Sure,' I said. "I was raising questions about what

Ann was wearing—wasn't wearing, actually. I'd seen Connie, Villeneuve, Mark Harnet and sister Louise together at the Salooon…"

"Uh huh," said Steve, "Guilt maketh paranoid." He paused and stretched to set his cup on the edge of the table. "It's still pretty speculative."

Mary glared at him. I cocked a thumb and shot him with my forefinger and he pretended to teeter on the verge of going over backwards in his chair and I went to the urn for a refill and on the way back, flipped on the lights. The day had been steadily going gray and I could tell from the clang of the halyards of the sailboats in the marina that the wind was rising.

"So what now?" I asked Mary.

"The ladies start looking through the returned checks tomorrow." She looked at her watch. "Right now, I've got to interview Frank Bullard, to see if he recognizes the shoe, and also to refresh my memory of the layout of his house."

Both Steve and I raised eyebrows, and Mary went on a little defiantly, "The guys at Heyoka Oceanic Technology found a few hairs and some sand in the shoe. They think the shoe could have floated from here to Flyaway Island within a month." She looked at Steve and me, "Good going, you two.

"I'm working on the theory that Ann may have overheard something and fled the house, before she could get both of her shoes and socks on. Maybe she was pursued. Perhaps she overheard something on an intercom or extension."

I asked about Louise's other brother, John Harnet, the dark-jowled tanker captain.

"His ship's in and loading," said Mary, "we'll get to him soon."

"If you're going to see Bullard," said Steve, "I think you should take a howitzer." But he was smiling as he pulled her up by the hand and said, "Come on, Marshall, I'll walk you to your cayuse before it gets blown away."

I watched them go hand in hand past the window, heads down against the wind.

Outside myself, the rap and clang of halyards was at an annoying level. The east wind was strong and gusty, the sky almost totally gray, just a thin line of blue far to the west. Offshore, an eastbound tanker tossed sheets of white from her bows as she bit into the rising sea.

No question, we were in for a blow—a stinking, New England Nor'easter.

THIRTY-TWO

THROUGH THE NIGHT THE WIND rose. By morning, sheets of rain were slapping the windows of the lighthouse. The reef over which I'd sailed was a jumble of suds. Out on Talon Rock a tree branch had snagged in the beacon and for an instant I took it to be someone stranded, waving wildly for rescue.

Arianna came up behind me and put her chin on my shoulder. "Gray day," she murmured. "Good day for work." She kissed me on the ear and put on her robe and went barefoot downstairs to the kitchen.

I dressed and we had a cup of coffee together and I left her, still in her robe, glaring at the screen of her computer. In the hall downstairs I got into storm regalia and, feeling like a yellow penguin, shuffled to the door. In an easterly wind the door is on the lee side of the tower, so I didn't have to fight to keep it from slamming open or struggle to close it after me, and was able to make a dignified entry into the maelstrom.

The marina is well protected from waves, but the masts of the sailboats were leaning over in the wind like groves of bamboo. Most of the sailors had tied off their halyards, and the clang of shackles against aluminum spars was virtually absent. There was just the basic screech of the wind and the roar of the waves; sounds so monotonous that my ears soon shut them out.

The dock lines on *Qvetchin' Gretchen* and *Buzzard* were doubled, so Tom and Steve had evidently gone on to work. The only signs of life were the faces and eyes of perhaps a dozen children, staring out the windows of their floating homes.

As I came to my two boats I saw their lines were as I'd left them, single. The sloop was dancing and *Hussar* was creaking against her fenders, but all was well. Perhaps the fact that Tom and Steve had not come by to double-rope my boats meant they figured I was okay and they could stop playing nurse. I sure hoped so.

I slid open the door on the lee side of the pilot house, went below and hung my foul-weather gear in the shower stall and was just setting the kettle on the stove when the phone rang. I scampered back to my office to get it before the machine.

"Hello."

"Hadrian? It's Roberta Richardson at HUG. Hear you're back in business."

"Yeah, Roberta, I guess I'm tougher than I look." I was glad to hear from her. Heyoka Underwriters Group is unusual in the industry—full of reasonable people who know boats. They pay well and they pay promptly.

"Can you handle an assignment? It's a rather odd

boat being sold to a sheik. We'd like you to look at it before we finalize things."

"How odd?" I asked.

"It's a World War Two PT boat, if you can believe it. I thought the last one of those sank under President Kennedy. What we'd like is it shouldn't sink under the sheik."

I didn't want to correct Roberta's grasp of history so I just said, "You mean *Taurus?* Owner Franklyn Bullard?"

"You got it," she said. "Bullard's an important customer around here—pays big premiums on his tankers. He's on his way to meet his new one the Centurion?...God, these rich people...so we're really under the gun. Is the PT there?"

"Not now. I think she's at the Sheldrake Shipyard for a bottom job."

"Good. We'd like some pictures of her running gear."

"Anything else?" I asked. The kettle was whistling.

"No, just the usual Underwriters Evaluation stuff: Is it gonna sink? Is it gonna burn? If all else fails, is there an anchor and a life raft? Take pictures so we have reason to believe the boat actually exists."

"When do you want it?" The kettle was screaming.

"Yesterday, naturally," I could see the smile on her big florid face. "Look, I know it's a shitty day but it's supposed to ease off later, at least for a while. Could you do it today?"

"Roberta, for you I'd climb the highest mountain." The kettle was now at full shriek.

"Great. I need this one."

"Okay, I'll look at it this afternoon and fax you a report in the morning. Bye now." I started to hang up, but she said, "Hey, wait a sec, there's a note on the back of this…"

I waited and then her voice continued, "Says here 'fuel tankage not to be more than fifteen hundred gallons.' Guess they don't want anyone trying to run this baby across the ocean. Any way you can check that?"

"I'll measure the tanks as carefully as I can and let you know what I think."

"Okey doke," she said and hung up.

I ran to the galley, killed the kettle and made a cup of coffee. Up in the pilot house, I mixed the brew with my favorite vice-looking out the window.

White triangles of foam flickered along the rim of the eastern breakwater and once in a while an entire wave heaved over and cascaded down the wall. Chunks of water from the tops of the waves that didn't get over the wall showered into the channel like stones.

Arianna was right: The only thing to do on a day like this was get to work.

THIRTY-THREE

BY THE TIME I GOT to Sheldrake in the mid afternoon, there were rifts of lighter gray in the clouds overhead. *Taurus* was inside the main shed alongside the skeleton of a partially plated aluminum sailboat. Two figures, masked and completely covered in white, were pouring what looked like blood from buckets into a drum while half a dozen other red-splattered mummies were stripping the masking tape from the waterline, gathering up the sheets of sandpaper strewn from bow to stern under the boat and clearing away the staging so that she could be launched.

The new red bottom paint looked sleek as eelskin. They might get another half-knot because of it.

I walked to the far end of the building, eyeing the scaffolds dangling from the distant rafters and the sparkling torches of the men plating the sailboat.

Up a long flight of swaying wooden stairs was the main office and there a brisk young woman with carrot hair and a faceful of freckles who was new to me, handed me the visitors' log to sign and gave me the keys to *Taurus,* all the while answering the phone and routing calls.

Down the rickety stairs I swayed once more, pausing halfway to get an overall photo of the deck. A minuscule yellow tractor began to pull the PT out of the shed and I had to scramble a bit to get my pictures.

The rain had tamed down to a drizzle and the wind to a light gale, so Manny and his crew were able to rig the slings and lift the boat without much of a struggle and I was able to get good close-up shots of the underwater running gear as they swung the boat over me and dropped her into the water.

As the launch crew were tying her up, Manny hopped out of the control shack and said, "If you're not done by quitting time, just drop the keys in the slot out front."

"Right you are, Manuel. The bottom looks great." With a grin, he gave me a thumbs-up and strode off, yellow slicker streaming, black boots squelching.

I usually begin work by doing the easy stuff first, so I took out my pocket tape recorder and walked over to the bridge and began making a list of the electronics. They were all set below a thick sheet of clear plexiglass which was open along the aft side for access to the control knobs and buttons. About the only thing unusual was there were two of everything, including radar. It seemed sensible; the hard ride of this big fast boat was bound to mean extra stress on connectors and circuit boards.

In the middle of the console was a large gyro compass and the screen of an electronic chart to continuously display course and position—nice when you're traveling fast. I also noticed the bows and white canvas of a dodger folded down in a gutter in the top of the bridge coaming. Stowing this way, it would be invisible from off the boat, but would shelter the driver on those days when he wasn't feeling hairy-chested and the boat was out of sight of land or the judges of a regatta.

I unlocked the companionway hatch and looked below. Canvas runners had been laid over the carpeting—a relief, because otherwise I'd have to take off my shoes and I hate working in my stocking feet. There are a zillion things in boats specifically designed to catch toes and crack shins.

The main electrical panel was behind the companionway ladder and I saw that the engine switches were off, but the house switch was on, so I flipped the toggle labeled Main Cabin and the lights came on. The galley was to the left behind a long counter of light wood with high-backed stools in front of it. There was a hi-lo convertible table of the same material in front of a long settee, two easy chairs at its ends. The bulkheads and the underside of the deck were egg-shell white, with varnished mahogany trim. The chair and settee cushions blue canvas with white piping. Bright and simple, verging on Spartan. I liked it. Ann liked splashy socks but, beyond those minor quirks, she was conservative, like most salts. She must have spent a lot of time crawling around with a tape-measure, color chips and fabric swatches to come up with something as elegant as this.

Forward and down a step were two cabins which shared the triangular head compartment in the very bow of the boat. Here I took up a main concern of the underwriters—is it going to sink?—and began looking at the boat's underwater inlets and outlets.

An hour later I had concluded the boat would float, and I had reached the engine compartment. In the gloom the two white engines looked like albino hippos browsing the bottom of a river.

I found the light switch and saw that the hippos' heads were the transmissions, now standing away from the engines themselves at the ends of necks that looked to be drive-shafts from heavy trucks. The twin Mitsubishi V-24 turbocharged diesels were spotless. The sumps underneath were fitted with long mirrors. "Sufficient unto the day is the power thereof," I muttered and gave the beasts a pat.

The only thing I didn't like the look of was a fuel hose on the top of the portside engine. It had apparently been made a little short and was bent very sharply around a corner of the air-intake mount. If it burst underway, fuel would spray into the air and run back along the underside of the deck to drip on the red-hot turbochargers and there'd be a dandy fire, possibly even an explosion. There were two large automatic Halon fire extinguishers on the bulkhead, but a fire at sea is a real heart-stopper—you can't solve it by running out into the street or dialing 911. Frank Bullard's skipper wouldn't like it, but that hose would have to be changed.

Between the engines was a stainless steel ladder to an overhead hatch onto the deck, and through a door in the aft end of the engine room was the compartment where the rudder shafts went through the bottom of the boat. Their bronze stuffing boxes looked a little green from minor seepage—but absolutely normal. There was a workbench back here too. A small safe stood under it along with several cases of oil and transmission fluid.

Now to the fuel tanks:

I turned and studied the fuel distribution panel on the forward bulkhead of the engine room. It was a straightforward arrangement of copper tubing and red-handled valves, arrayed on each side of the ladder into the compartment and easy to understand with just a few minutes study. The two tanks must be forward of the bulkhead, under the floor of the passageway from the main saloon. There was a circular aluminum manhole in the face of the bulkhead under the ladder, but I hoped there would be another, easier access-panel in the floor of the passageway.

The passageway was floored with varnished

wooden tiles and I flipped back the canvas drop cloth and found another circular aluminum plate like the one under the stairs of the engine room. The lid had a recessed handle; half a turn and it unlocked and lifted off easily. I found myself looking at the aft faces of two large aluminum tanks. The bottom of the compartment was the top of the keel and it was covered with water. The water was clear, no trace of oil or fuel, the compartment as clean as the engine room.

With a sigh, I set my toolbox down, took off my shoes and socks, rolled up my cuffs and lowered myself in.

The water was cool. I wiggled my toes to adjust, dipped a finger in and tasted it—fresh. Probably a leak in the plumbing for the faucets and showers.

The tanks were wedge-shaped and butted against a vertical plywood panel that ran fore-and-aft between the keel and the underside of the passageway. Another bulkhead ran across the compartment and rose about halfway up and a few inches behind the ends of the tanks. I'd be able to push my tape measure down the gap to get one of the dimensions I'd need to calculate how much fuel they'd carry.

Looking for signs or smells of seeps or oozes I shone my flashlight into the space between the passageway floor and the tops of the tanks and studied the fill, vent and supply lines. There was a light coating of dust on the tops of the tanks and something rectangular—maybe a case of oil—had evidently been stowed at one time on the starboard tank. Otherwise, everything looked clean and dry, all the hoses were fire-resistant, mesh reinforced hose with heavy-duty end fittings.

I moved on to look at the aft flanges of the tanks. The gap between the half-bulkhead and the back ends of the tanks was only about two inches, but by jamming my head right against the tank I found I could peer one-eyed along the entire flange. The lip of the port tank was clean, bright metal right around, but down in the vee of the low corner of the starboard tank my light found a red sock.

"Omigod." And I fell on my butt into the bilge-water.

THIRTY-FOUR

I PULLED MYSELF ONTO MY knees and forced my arm into the gap, but the red sock was beyond the ends of my fingers. I needed a tool, a stick, a wire coat hanger—but the hangers I'd seen in the cabins were molded plastic. I splashed aft on my knees, pushed out the manhole in the engine room bulkhead and slithered under the stairs. I yanked the oil bayonet out of the port engine and scrambled back to the tank the way I had come. The dipstick was a steel blade about an inch wide and three feet long, curled at the top to form a finger-pull and it was dripping black oil. I wiped it by dragging it between my sleeve and side, and then found that neither the curled nor pointed end would catch the sock. I grabbed the pliers from my toolbox and pried open the finger-pull to make a hook and caught the sock on the first try. Heart pounding, I stood up in the manhole and held the sock to the light. There was the white letter P. It had to be Ann's. But how in the devil...

"What the hell are you doing on this boat, Wallace?"

It was the other brother, the dark-jowled captain of tankers.

"Er, ah." I tried to whip the sock out of sight below the rim of the hatch, but he'd seen it and he lunged.

I ducked down and he skidded by. I popped back up as he pounded toward me on his knees, shoving the manhole cover in front of him to decapitate me. He was smiling, a man happy in his work.

I saw red. Who did this homicidal Hun think he was anyway? I slashed at him with the dipstick, holding it two-handed like a broadsword. He screamed and grabbed the side of his head. The hook must have torn his ear because instantly blood was soaking his shoulder and splattering the floor. He lunged at me, but slipped in his blood. I ducked and scrambled aft into the engine room. I heard him, scrabbling and puffing, trying to get traction, and I fled up the ladder to the deck, cracking my head on the center dog of the hatch as I hurled myself through it. The clouds, wind and rain were back, making it dark enough for cars on the street to have their lights on. The yard was closed. There was no one in sight.

I leapt for the dock and almost flipped into the water as my feet went from under me. Harnet appeared and ran toward the bow to cut me off at the ramp, but I made it just ahead of him when he tripped on a cleat. I raced up the ramp and toward my car with him snorting behind me.

He was tiring and I gained enough time to drop my keys, grovel, come up with my nose in the license plate of the car behind mine—Y-KNOT!—get in and lock the doors before he reached me. Bleeding, panting, one hand to his head, the other on the hood of the Y-KNOT car, he stared at me, hollow-eyed, done in. As I screeched away, he collapsed across the hood of his car, head in his arms.

"I hope he bleeds to death."

THIRTY-FIVE

"I ARRIVED AT HEYOKA POLICE headquarters shoeless, sockless, shaking, sopping wet and dripping blood from this gash," I bent my head to show Arianna the maroon oval in my hairline, "which till then I hadn't even noticed."

She was gazing at me with a mixture of wonder and relief and seemed to be on the verge of either tears or laughter. After a moment she settled on a wry-fond smile, tucked her legs up under her on the new beige sofa that had arrived a scant hour before me and asked, "Was Mary there?"

"No, but the Inspector was and the others rushed around, found these dry clothes…" I flapped an arm of the oversized dark-blue coveralls which made me feel like a scarecrow…"and these boots…" Arianna and I studied the gleaming, red-leather gunboats on my feet. "These are evidently the Inspector's—at least they came from the closet in her office." I held out a leg and turned the boot from side to side. "About all I can say is the lady has a mind of steel, a heart of gold—and feet as big as Texas. I'm swimming in these things!"

Arianna settled into the opposite corner of the sofa The ice in her Scotch tinkled as she absentmindedly poked the top cube. "How do you suppose the sock got there—in the bilge of the boat?"

I pulled in a stream of vodka and collected my wits.

"You know, I think the sock got there because Ann was in the fuel-tank compartment, much as I was, and she probably took off her shoes and socks too, because of the bilge water."

"Hadrian, wouldn't she have just left them on the floor outside the hatch? You said that's what you did."

"Sure, but suppose she heard someone come on board and she didn't want to be found there."

"Why not? It's her boat," said Arianna.

"Yeah," I said. "The only thing I've thought of is she was looking for another computer disk to replace the one she'd dropped off the bridge."

Arianna prodded the ice in her drink with a pink fingernail. She looked as though she were going to interrupt, but then changed her mind with a smile and said, "Maybe I'd just better hear the whole hypothesis, professor."

"Well, you know, the space on top of the fuel tanks would be a pretty good hiding place, say for a briefcase containing a back-up copy of Louise's check-making program. You could get in there quickly to retrieve it, but you'd really have to be doing a hard search to find it."

Arianna stared blankly at me for a moment and then murmured, "Would she do that? It doesn't sound like a place you'd be likely to go in the course of decorating a boat."

I smiled. "You never sailed with her. She was very interested in the machinery and technical stuff. I remember once on a trip across the Atlantic..."

"All right, all right," said Arianna.

I sensed I'd better stick to the immediate details of Ann's life and death.

"I think Ann found the briefcase—or whatever it was—earlier, took a disk, tried it out at home and found it didn't make sense—remember she asked me if computers were used on boats?"

"Yes. Go on."

I glanced out the window at the sky. Nearly dark; a thin rain sticking to the glass, leaving marks like tiny animal feet.

"She may have been coming to show it to me, but had to ditch it because Frank appeared—it would be awkward to tell him where she was going and why. I don't remember pockets in her shirt. It was more or less translucent, you know."

"I don't," said Arianna wryly. "But you evidently do."

I quickly took a swig of vodka.

"So, she went to the boat to get another disk?"

"That's the way I see it," I said. Someone probably came to get the disks that same weekend, because the boat was scheduled to be moved to Sheldrake for its engines. Ann was unlucky enough to be on the boat when whoever it was arrived to get the disks off the boat."

"I think I see," said Arianna. "She hears or senses from the movement of the boat that someone's come aboard, she grabs her shoes and socks, closes the hatch and hunkers down in there with the tanks."

"And whatever she found," I added.

"Yes," said Arianna. "And the hand holding the socks is resting on the top of that half-partition just behind the tanks and… And then what?"

"If she found a briefcase," I said, "I see her opening it, grabbing another disk and shoving the case back. The rectangle I saw in the dust on top of the tank was a little ragged around the edges."

"Yes, I see. That's when the socks get adrift. One drops in the gap when she puts the case back… She scoops up her shoes and the remaining sock, starts to put them on. The hatch is opened by whomever and she scurries into the engine room by the same route you did."

Fingering my dented forehead, I said, "Captain Harnet and I may have replayed the event. Except Ann was stunned and went on overboard and drowned."

"Perhaps it was Louise and the fiery Ms. Maladetta?"

I looked at the garish boots on my feet and at the rain, heavy now and making runnels on the black window. I would prefer not to believe it of Connie. Still, it could be the truth." I drained my drink.

"In any case," I continued. "I'm now virtually certain it was one of the Harnet brothers who attacked me at the cemetery."

Arianna raised an eyebrow. "You're thinking of the license plate?"

"It's more than that. On the drive home, I remembered something about the attacker."

"Oh?"

"She had a prominent Adam's apple. That's not a normal female feature." I fingered my slightly knobby neck and glanced at her smooth one.

Arianna had kicked off the moccasins she normally wore around the house and her bare toes and heels left catlike marks in the new carpet, a hand-woven traditional Heyoka pattern of interlocking circles in blue, red and yellow. She was wearing a light blue button-down shirt and faded jeans which fit snugly only across the seat, and I pondered yet again the mysterious power of a winsome butt. No doubt moths have similar feelings about flames.

She came back with fresh drinks and a thoughtful look. "Do you know what this is like, what we've been doing here?"

I didn't understand and I shook my head.

"It's like collaborating on a book. I did that once. You sit around and spin scenes until you have something you like. Then you write it down."

"I see," I said. "You're saying it's kind of thin."

"No, not at all. It's believable." Arianna gave one cube a flick and the whole clump spun slowly in the amber liquid. "And very sad."

"I guess we'll know soon enough," I said. "Once the women at the station heard my tale, they sprang to the phones like a posse to horse. The last thing the Inspector said was, 'Go home, Mr. Wallace. We'll take it from here.'"

THIRTY-SIX

NEAR DAWN THE RAIN STOPPED and we woke to gray clouds racing close overhead. The wind whined and hissed around the window frames. Arianna and I nestled, savoring our comfort, neither wanting to face the dismal morning.

But I had promised a report to the insurance company and Arianna gets cranky if she doesn't manage at least one page of manuscript a day, so we finally levered ourselves out of bed and to our duties. I left her glaring into the gray glow of her word processor, robed and barefoot, coffee in one hand and an apple in the other.

At the marina the docks and walkways were undulating, the boats dancing under the gusty wind, but these were the only signs of life. A lot of folks habitually went inland to wait storms out.

The rain roared in again just as I reached my boat. Head down, I scrambled into the pilot-house and went below to set the kettle on for a second cup of coffee. The phone began to ring and I reached it just as the answering machine picked up.

"Hadrian? It's Roberta at HUG."

"Hang on while I turn off the tape." I punched the button.

"Can you work today?"

"You said you wanted the report pronto, so here I am."

"Well, it's a lousy day. It's not supposed to last long, but it's gonna be vicious, and I thought you might not be able to work."

"It's not that bad here, the marina's reasonably well protected," I said and stood up to look out a porthole at the surf exploding on the eastern breakwater.

"That's good to hear. We're under even more pressure because the deal's done and the Sheik wants to take it as soon as the weather clears. Usually the underwriters want a full-fledged survey with trials and everything when a boat changes hands, but they'll take the boat if your report's clean."

"It's clean," I said. "Couple of clamps and a new fuel hose is all I spotted. And there's some sort of a leak in the fresh-water system; probably minor." I didn't know if what was going on with the police investigation might affect the sale or the insurance, but I didn't think I could spill police business, so I did a quick mental calculation and said, "Given the space under the sole and between the bulkheads, the tankage must be very close to fifteen hundred—near as never mind, anyway."

"When do you think you'll fax the written report?"

"About two hours."

"Good going, Hade. And thanks. You can bill at the extra rate, for super-service." "Extra rate" was Roberta's code to tell me it was okay to pad the bill a bit as a reward for service beyond the call.

"Hey, thanks!"

"Not at all. You busted your ass on this one, and I appreciate it."

AN HOUR AND A HALF later I had finished the report. I put the kettle on, went back to my computer, and clicked the icons to send the report. The computer screen soon showed transmission in progress, so I walked back to the galley, spooned coffee into a mug and set it in the sink while I went to the head. As I stepped over the sill, the kettle started to whine and the phone rang.

It never fails.

I supposed it was Roberta calling to ask a question or say she'd gotten the fax, so I finished my pee and turned off the kettle before getting the phone. The answering machine was running, but instead of hearing Roberta when I picked up the receiver, it was Manny Arecibo saying, "...took off out of here like a bat, sank two boats on the way out and he's probably dragging a mooring on one propeller."

"Manny, what in hell are you taking about?"

"Hadrian? Is that you?"

"Si, si, amigo, que pasa?"

"Three Heyoka police women showed up about an

hour ago and the PT fired up and shot out of here. Went straight through the moored boats, sank…"

"Okay, Manny, I heard that on the machine."

"The cops piled into their cars to see if they could get a shot at them as they passed the condos. One of the cops—Mary?—said I should call you and tell you to try to intercept them."

In this weather? Who did Mary think I was, Wolf Larsen? *The Flying Dutchman?* I took a deep breath and steadied myself by sitting down.

"What about the Coast Guard? They've got a two-hundred-foot cutter stationed at Riversend on Eskar Island. That's halfway up the sound."

"We tried already. They're on a search-and-rescue way out in the Hudson Canyon since dawn."

My stomach fell like a cannon ball. "Did the PT go up sound or down?"

"Up. To you," said Manny. "I climbed the crane and saw them turn east. They're not going very fast. I think they snagged a mooring chain, maybe the whole damn mooring, on a prop."

If Manny could climb that crane in this stuff, I guessed I could fire up *Hussar* and at least maybe tail them until the gale was over and the police or Coast Guard could loft a helicopter gunship.

"Okay, Manuel, I'll try. Who's aboard?"

"Skipper, a thin girl, a tall woman—black hair, big eyes…"

"I know who it is, Manny. How much fuel do they have?"

A pause as Manny ruminated. "No new fuel since the trials. They were run at half load. Might be down to four, maybe five hundred gallons."

"What did she weigh when you launched her?"

"Just on forty-five tons."

I calculated: Fifteen hundred gallons of diesel would weigh just about six tons. Fueled full, the boat probably weighed about fifty tons, so Manny was probably right. *Taurus* might only have a few hours running in her. Probably try to make it to Bullard's new tanker, turn it around, and get out of the country.

I turned on the radio and tried the intership channels… Static.

"Manny tell the police, I'll go out and do what I can, but they have to send help just as soon as they can. I'll have the radio on channel seventy-eight."

"Go get 'em, Hadrian," said Manny, and he hung up.

I took a quick look in the engine compartment and then rushed up to the wheel-house and looked around:

Gray sky, gray rain, gray waves; even the spume looked gray. Gray docks swaying on gray water. No lights in any boat. The parking lot full of gulls hunkered down to wait it out. No people. The phone was always off at Arianna's when she was working and with everything I had to do to get the boat going there was no time to get her.

Oshit. Not a moment to lose, and no one in sight.

THIRTY-SEVEN

I GOT THE BURNERS AFIRE and dialed the lighthouse. The phone was on message. I hopped from one foot to the other until it gave a beep, then I grated out a compressed bulletin which basically said HELP! I hung up and quickly redialed. I could tell I'd successfully overridden the machine when the rings went beyond four. I put the phone down on the desk—maybe the repetitive burr of noise from the phones in the house would get past her concentration or she'd get up to stretch or have a cup of coffee and hear it then.

I ran forward and ignored a lot of the niceties as I rushed to disconnect all the shoreside wires and plumbing except the phone jack. I just left everything where it fell—on the dock or into the water.

I tore back into the wheel house to check on the steam—the main gauge was off the pin—and as I came back out to start detaching the mooring lines I caught the orange flash of Arianna's foul-weather gear amid the trees and saw her running for the footbridge.

I started taking off the extra lines and when I came to the phone jack again, found it was stuck. I kicked it. It came apart, the red, green, black and yellow wires springing out like the guts of a shrimp.

As Arianna slid to a stop beside me, there was a dazzling flash and we watched a lightning bolt strike the water out beyond the breakwaters and saw a boiling black cloud charging toward us. We scampered into the boat and I slammed the door as a solid mass of water fell. We waited beneath the roar, feeling like two passengers on a train thundering through a tunnel, not even trying to talk. Then the rain was gone.

The gray light of day came back and Tom was on the dock, an Alp in yellow, water running like brooks through the creases of his slicker and falling in solid streams from his elbows and cuffs. Next to Tom stood Alice Emeu, a molehill to his mountain, clad not in yellow, but purple, a color I never before saw in seagoing gear.

"What's up, Hadrian?" she shouted.

"I've got to get the boat out and I haven't got time to explain."

"Okay, you can explain on the way," and she hopped onto the first step of the boarding platform.

"You're going out in this?" yelled Tom, and it was hard to say whether he was more nonplussed by the sight of Alice skipping up the stairs or the prospect of leaving the dock.

"Tom. I've got to. Handle the spring lines. I'll fill you in on the way. Alice, you can't come."

Alice Emeu turned furious black eyes on me. "Listen, pup, I've been driving boats since before your grandmother had the hankers..." The wind wiped a lot of her words away, but as she mounted the stairs I also heard, "Haven't been out in a smoker like this since I was a girl... Had a rescue station here then..." She was actually grinning as she stepped across the sill and into the pilot house, waggled a hand at Arianna and growled at me, "Come on, Cap, we're wasting time."

I looked out at Tom and Tom looked in at me and... What could we do? We shrugged.

With Tom on the dock handling the lines and me backing the prop and using maximum thruster we managed to peel *Hussar* away from the dock, although I gave the stern a terrific wallop on the last piling when I forced her into the turn too soon.

As we ran down the channel between the breakwaters, spray rattled against the sides and windows of the wheelhouse and the wind heeled us to starboard. I filled my crew in as we went, Tom and Alice calmly studied the waves to windward and Arianna clutched the brass guard rail of the instrument panel, tendons of her knuckles showing sharp.

The tide was very high, made so by the combination of the strong easterly wind and low barometric pressure. The breakwaters were reefs, just awash; we could see right over them.

"What do you think it's blowing?" I asked Tom.

"There are long streaks of foam on the backs of most of the waves. Must be thirty to thirty-five, forty in the gusts."

"With embedded thunderstorms," I added, thinking of the lightning bolt and the huge dump of water we'd taken just before Tom and Alice appeared.

"Yeah, skipper, 'tis a fairly foul day' all right," said Tom with a grin.

"Have you ever had *Hussar* out in weather like this, Hadrian?" asked Arianna.

"No."

She turned her gaze forward again.

My answer didn't seem to concern Alice or Tom much, but it did me. Had it simply been a question of riding out the storm, I'd have known what to do—motor slowly into it and wait for it to blow over. Actually, *Hussar* could probably slice directly into a head sea at any speed I chose, like a surfaced submarine. But the PT was to our right and would be coming up the middle of the sound; there was no lee on either shore. To cross her path, I had to get out there, and that meant *Hussar* had to take the waves at an angle from the left, almost on her port beam. They just might roll us over.

Tom had turned on the electronics and as he finished tuning the radar, I said, "I told Manny we'd be listening on channel seventy eight on the radio."

He punched the numbers into the key pad then turned to me and said, "How are you going to play it?"

I pushed the throttle to bring the needles in the gauges vertical and said, "I'll set her for twelve knots and see if we can take the seas broad on the port bow. That'll take us toward the middle and also eastward up the sound, the same direction he's going."

"Sounds good," Tom said and, eyeing the foaming end of the breakwater as we came up to it, "Here we go."

I started the turn before we were out from the shelter of the eastern breakwater but even so the first wave laid us so far down I thought it was all over. Alice and Tom were practically horizontal against the starboard pilot house door, Arianna lost her footing and hung from the handrail like a gymnast. I dangled likewise from the steering wheel.

I managed to get my feet onto the normally vertical bar of the gear lever and slowly forced the wheel to port. My old boat came around and righted and I soon found we could all keep our feet with the steam gauges at one o'clock and the seas about thirty degrees on the bow. The loran and GPS both showed us doing eight knots over the bottom. The foredeck was pretty sudsy most of the time. Often, the only part of the boat visible above the froth was the yellow pennant at the stemhead. From outside we probably did look like a submarine running awash.

Inside it was bearable. With all the windows and ports shut we found we could talk in a moderate shout, but no matter how high we turned the volume we could not hear the radio. So we shut it off. There was so much flying water and we were so low down relative to the waves that the radar screen showed nothing but a jumbled hash, so Tom finally shut if off too.

After we'd been punching along in the gray for about an hour, there came a strange and lovely moment: the clouds thinned and the air brightened and we were lifted high by a particularly large wave. The sea looked like acres of white flowers, thrashing wildly under the wind and tossing petals to the sky.

But mostly what we saw was low gray cloud scudding swiftly by, the thin black band of the distant shore, and ranks and ranks of waves marching endlessly at us.

Our bow would slide into an oncoming wall of foam-laced water until the yellow banner was nearly submerged. *Hussar* would shudder and pause while all the forces—the forward thrust of the propeller, the backward thrust of the wave; the downward drive of the hull and the upwelling of the sea—fused in balance. We'd lift, roll to the right; up would come the foredeck, carrying a transparent hill of water. The hill would explode, roar aft, thump halfway up the windows of the pilot house, then hiss into the walkways and cascade over the sides. Free of that wave, we'd roll to the left and thrust into the next one.

And so we went, edging toward the middle of the sound as best we could, our four pairs of eyes scanning gray seas for a gray boat.

Well, three pairs, actually. My eyes were watching another squall build and race toward us. First it was a black streak far away and looked much like the shoreline; but it was directly to the east where there was no land. It rapidly thickened and stretched out to the sides; I saw sparkles of lightning in it.

I tapped Tom on the shoulder and pointed forward. He looked, nodded and passed the word. Everyone got ready to hang on tighter and went back to scanning their sector of the sea—Alice to port; Tom to starboard; Arianna beside me, looking ahead.

The edge of the black cloud swept over us with a roar and a flash, and the boat rang as bars of solid water crashed down on us. The wheel house went black except for the dim red lights of the engine gauges and the compass. I edged left to a heading of due east to face squarely into it, and we swayed along in a rumbling black cavern, waiting for the thing to pass over.

The tons of falling water had the effect of flattening the sea and I noticed the speed creeping up toward twelve, the usual tempo for the throttle setting. As the speed went up, the rolling went down. It seemed like a good time to feed the crew. We'd been out almost three hours.

I grabbed Tom and pulled him over to the wheel and pointed to the white E on the compass. In the glow from the compass he made the okay sign and took the wheel. Below, I put the kettle on and started handing up loaves of bread and packages of cheese. They were snatched from my fingers. I ranged four mugs in the sink, got the top off a jar of coffee and shook some into each cup with one hand while hanging on with the other.

While I waited for the kettle to show steam, I looked in the bilge and checked the fuel: an inch of water, a foot of kerosene. The amount of water was normal. One foot of fuel meant about four hours, running at this speed. Mark Harnet in *Taurus* might be down to about half that time.

Steam was gushing from the kettle. I slopped boiling water at the cups until I had them three-quarters full, more or less. Then I lifted them one by one into the companionway where they too were snatched away.

I came up into a wheel house that smelled of bread, cheese and coffee and gleamed with a lively flash of teeth and eyes. It was noticeably lighter and Tom pointed forward to a thin gray line in the gloom. The line thickened into a band that separated sea and cloud, the rain—if you could call the free-fall of liquid we'd been under mere rain—the rain stopped. The final shreds of black cloud flew away astern and we were once more in a gray wasteland.

"There's our boy," said Alice, and she put her arm against Arianna's shoulder, pointing ahead and to the right.

The PT boat was about a quarter of a mile away, slamming into it, great fans of spray sheeting from her bows.

"Man's in a hurry," said Tom.

"He must have seen us," said Alice, eyes glowing with the heat of the chase.

As we watched, *Taurus* reared on the back of a wave and tilted over the crest, exposing her rudders and propellers.

"Something funny about that portside prop," said Tom.

As the PT went over the next crest and the stern came clear of the water, I saw what he meant—the starboard propeller was a silver circle, but the port one looked like it had a black hole in the middle of the whirling disk.

I took the wheel from Tom. He picked the binoculars from their rack. The next time *Taurus* crested a wave, Tom said, "There's a lot of rusty chain wrapped around it."

"That's what slowed him up," I said.

"The wind's down," said Tom and I saw he was right. The tide had turned, carrying the sea into the wind, so the waves were wicked; but the gale was definitely winding down. We were able to talk at a shout.

"Can we catch him?" asked Arianna. We were all crowded against the control panel, looking forward, our bodies rubbing, our slickers squeaking as we rolled and swayed with the boat.

"Probably not," I said, "But we can press him. Make him use fuel faster. Slamming like that, maybe something will break." I shoved the throttle forward and watched the needles rise to three o'clock on the dials—maximum cruise.

Hussar charged the waves, carrying our yellow banner quivering into them. She ran steadier at this speed, her bow higher. From below came a singing whine that rose as we slashed into a wave and died away as we burst through to tear down its forward slope.

"What's that noise?" Tom shouted in my ear.

"The shaft binding in its bearings as the hull twists," I shouted back.

"Is it okay?" Tom was frowning. He'd never been aboard at this speed in conditions like these. Neither had I.

"Oh, yeah," I shouted. "The bearings are water-cooled and there's lots of grease in 'em too."

Tom looked at Alice and Arianna and lifted his shoulders. They just smiled—Alice broadly, Arianna bravely—and turned their attention back to the fleeing warboat.

Tom turned on the radar and adjusted it. After a few moments he said, "We're gaining."

The screen was eyed eagerly by Alice, a ninety-pound tigress yearning for the kill.

We continued to forge ahead, and gained enough for me to clearly see the golden bull stretched across the PT's transom. The driver of the PT had the dodger up, and was in full yellow oilskins too. He rarely looked back and I guessed he was seeing all he needed on his radar screen.

On we thrashed, the PT boat bucking and slamming over the waves, we barreling through, barreling after *Taurus* like a torpedo.

But as the wind fell, the waves shrank and the warboat began to pull away. Our speed increased too, till the loran showed nineteen over the bottom and the GPS 18, but *Taurus* continued to gain and by the time we raised Flyaway Island, the PT was halfway between us and the horizon. Whenever one of the larger waves came along, we'd lose sight of her.

Nobody said anything, but the cabin seemed gloomier than it had at the height of the blackest squalls.

We continued to churn along and Tom continued to watch the radar and suddenly he said, "We're gaining again!"

The women clustered around the screen, balancing by holding on to each other and I could sense the battle lust rising even in Arianna as they alternately eyed the screen and the forward window.

We were, in fact, gaining, and rapidly. Soon we could see the PT was wallowing sideways in the waves and we watched a yellow figure crawl aft toward the engine room hatch.

"What's happened, Hadrian?" It was Alice, able to stand unsupported behind me now. "May have used up his fuel," I said.

Tom had the glasses up and said, "He's doing something alongside that big ventilator aft. Looks like he's tugging on a lever."

"Tom, he's had a fire!" I said. "The boat's got an automatic Halon system. It shuts off the engines and closes the air scoops if there's a fire because diesels will ingest Halon and once it's gone, the fire may break out again. Harnet's reopening the main air scoop so he can restart. I think a fuel hose burst on the port one." I explained what I'd seen when I'd looked the boat over for HUG.

"We're catching him fast now," Tom said. "What are you going to do?"

"Ram him," I said. "Put a hole in him before he can get going again." I gave the throttle a smack with the palm of my hand to make sure it was all the way to the stops and as I did, the safety valve let go with a shriek.

"Damn and shit!" I yelled as we crashed through several waves and turned sideways to the sea ourselves. Alice had fallen down and everyone else was hanging onto the handrails.

Through the windshield I saw Harnet scramble back under the dodger; then a great gout of purple smoke shot out of the starboard exhaust.

"Tom, he's got an engine going. Can you get the valve reset?"

Tom was already on his way, snatching the gloves from under the settee as he went. We were rolling so deeply that I didn't think he could do it, but he did.

When he had the valve closed I pushed the orange lever on the control panel and locked the valve shut. Through the window I had seen the PT boat get underway and go into a wide turn, banking way over like a fighter plane lining up to strafe. No time for safety now, I had to get steam up and no kidding around about it. If I didn't, Harnet was going to put us deep down under.

I pushed all the levers for all the burners to their stops and the four of us watched the main steam gauge.

It came off the pin after a few eons and I began to feed steam to the bow thruster and the engine as fast as I could and still keep the needle rising. I couldn't sense any forward motion in the boat.

Outside, the PT had finished its turn and was and coming at us, blood-red bottom making an evil grin.

The compass showed our bow beginning to swing before I could sense it, but once started, it moved faster and faster. The tachometer showed the shaft turning at ten, twenty, thirty-two, forty-five RPM. I held the rudder hard to its stops and watched the compass. Come on, come on, come on.

Harnet must have lost sight of us behind his bow and not realized we were turning to face him. I saw the bow of the PT boat waggle as he hunted for us in the last moments.

But he was too late. *Hussar* had come around and was waiting for him like a planted pike. Our metal met his plywood. The bow staff carrying our yellow pennant curled backward and vanished in a shower of splinters as *Hussar* went in unto old *Taurus* like a rapier into a shoe box.

THIRTY-EIGHT

WE GRATED TO A STOP with the edge of the PT boat's deck about fifteen feet from our wheel house. Harnet had been thrown through the window of the dodger and was splayed out, face down, on the foredeck.

Tom looked at me with a question in his eyes.

"Think you can get over there and kill the engine or at least get it out of gear?" I asked.

"Sure," he said, and started off. I thought of something else. "See if you can also figure out how to close the main air scoop back aft. It'll help keep her afloat."

"Gotcha," he said and pulled open the pilot house door. Fresh air flooded in as Tom, arms outstretched to balance himself, ran onto the deck of the sinking PT.

The two boats were rolling and grinding a little, but it wasn't too bad. The opposing thrust of the two engines was holding the boats together and causing us to circle slowly to the right. The wind was virtually gone and the waves were mostly just swells now, largish, but without white caps. The current had carried us a couple of miles farther along toward Flyaway Island and there was a nick on the horizon in that direction that might be help on its way, or might be Bullard in his new tanker or the other Harnet in his. I remembered Mary saying the murderous—and now possibly earless—Harnet's ship had been loading. Perhaps he'd made it to sea before the posse back in Heyoka were fully mounted up.

On the PT, Mark Harnet raised himself on his arms and stared at me. His normally hawk-sharp face looked stunned and mild and very pale. Blood dripped from his nose and mouth.

I turned around to Alice and Arianna and said, "Look, I've got to go over there and see to him and find the others."

"I'll come with you," said Arianna.

"Okay. Alice, just keep the throttle where it is until we give you the sign that Tom has shut the PT's engine down or got her out of gear. Then move this brass lever to the right and take us out of gear."

"Aye, aye, Cap," she said with a twinkle in her eye and a cocky salute. She grabbed the wheel.

I rummaged in the drawer under the settee until I found a bag of plastic electrical ties, then I took Arianna's hand and we climbed onto the bow of *Taurus*.

The skipper was on his back now, eyes closed, his

face mottled. I slipped a tie around each wrist and pulled them together with a third.

"Harnet, can you hear me?"

No reaction.

"Lie still. We'll get you off in a minute." There was a raspy gurgle and blood oozed from his mouth onto the deck.

Tom came up. "The engine's died and I got the vent closed, Hade, but air's rushing out all over her. She won't last long."

I signaled Alice to take *Hussar* out of gear and said, "Tom, you get Harnet off. Put him in my cabin and lock the door. Arianna and I will look below."

Tom tucked Harnet under one arm and jumped onto *Hussar*. I climbed down the PT's companionway stairs, followed by Arianna.

Hussar had punched through Taurus' port bow at a slight angle. As we came down the ladder we saw the port side of my boat, her bow had smashed right on through the main bulkhead of the PT and was invisible; I doubted it was much hurt. Louise Harnet was sitting on the cabin floor up to her waist in seawater, deathly pale, and obviously in great pain. Her right arm was wrapped in a blood-soaked towel which Connie Maladetta was trying to tie up with panty hose. Arianna waded over to them, squatted down and helped.

A number of tan plastic bags were piled on the settees; some had burst and spilled money into the water. The water was streaked with Louise's blood and rising fast.

Tom's head appeared in the companionway. "How's it going down there?"

"Not too good. Give us a hand with Louise."

Tom hung from the front edge of the companionway and dropped into the cabin with a splash. He sloshed over to Louise, cradled her in his arms and surged up the ladder. Arianna, Connie and I followed right after him.

I had one of the tan bags, and as I came out on deck the bag jammed in a corner of the companionway. I tugged; it tore. Banded bricks of cash splashed into the rising water below.

"Get a move on," I said, and Arianna, Connie and I more or less hurled ourselves onto *Hussar.* Tom passed Louise to us and nearly went over the side, but he managed to catch the last unmangled stanchion on our foredeck. It bent under him and he landed aboard with a thump.

Taurus was far down at the stern now, and I reversed *Hussar* at full throttle. We came away with a screech, a crack and a shower of new splinters as our stem ripped through six feet of the PT boat's deck.

Water rushed into the hole we'd occupied and the bow began to settle. Soon she was riding more or less level with her deck about a foot above the surface of the sea. Bubbles streamed from the many fractures all over her. There were loud gurgles and an occasional gush of spray from the open companionway.

I studied the depth finder. The flashing light on the whirring dial showed just a little over sixty feet and spiky points of light scattered around the dial indicated a rocky bottom, so the tidal currents shouldn't move her much. I looked at the loran and the GPS, and wrote the coordinates in the logbook.

I sighted across the compass and wrote down the bearing to the highest part of Flyaway Island. Probably ought to put a marker buoy down too. "Tom…"

"Ship coming, Hadrian," he said. I looked up and saw a huge black vessel to port, pushing a glassy hill of water before her.

"Uh oh."

Alice had the glasses to her eyes. "It's name is *HMS Centurion*. Like Commodore Anson's ship. My, my."

"How's that, Alice?"

"Hadrian, surely you remember Anson. He captured a Spanish treasure galleon off Manila in…" she paused, "Oh, around 1740 and brought home a simply enormous amount of gold and silver. Maybe something like a billion dollars in today's terms. His ship was *HMS Centurion*."

I jumped and grabbed Alice, making Tom and Arianna stare. "Of course!" I cried, "The taking of the Golden Galleon!" And right then, I knew what Frank Bullard was up to; where there was enough money to interest him. The surge of triumph made me so dizzy, I dropped onto the settee.

"Tom," I don't remember the HMS on your model."

"It wasn't." Bullard said it would spoil the look of the bow. He said he might have to paint Heyoka Motor Ship on his tanker, but there was no law that said he had to put it on his model."

We studied Frank Bullard's oncoming behemoth and finally Tom said, "Doesn't look like he's got anything hostile in mind."

"Yeah, well, him we can outrun," I said. Let's see if he's on the radio. My hands were shaking as I stood and twisted the knob. The dial lighted, but neither voice nor static came out.

Tom stuck his head out the door and said, "The antenna's gone. Maybe lightning hit it?" I shrugged and switched the radio off.

HMS Centurion plowed on and began to pass about fifty yards away. Taurus was awash now, swaying gently, an occasional wave rolling right across her foredeck, air hissing and belching from her ventilators and the companionway hatch. Frank Bullard stepped out on the bridge wing with a megaphone in his hand. He put it to his mouth and roared, "Wallace?"

I cupped my hands and shouted, "Yes, Bullard?"

"The Sheik's not going to like this."

"Well, boo hoo," I yelled. "Boo hoo hoo!"

The bow wave of the tanker reached *Taurus,* rolled across her. Blood, water and greenbacks gushed from the open companionway and the old gray warboat descended into the cold gray sea.

Frank Bullard eyed the bubbles and the rafts of cash for a moment, then put the horn to his lips and bellowed:

"Right. To hell with him." He looked again at where *Taurus* had gone down. "Anyone hurt?"

"Yes, but not fatally." I now had reason to suspect he'd hoped otherwise.

"Do you need help? I can't stop this thing, but we can radio ahead."

"You do that. Ask for ambulances at the Flyaway Shipyard. We'll make it that far all right."

Frank left the bridge. I could practically hear him on the radio: Good old unsuspecting, paternal Frank Bullard, shocked, Shocked! by people he'd trusted and treated like family.

The black ship slid away, a toad upon the waters. *Hussar* shivered in her wake. I glared at the spot on the tanker's bridge where I'd last seen Frank Bullard. "Meatface, I've gotcha now!"

THIRTY-NINE

"THERE WE WERE with the PT boat awash and *Hussar* spouting water from every pump…and when Alice mentioned Commodore Anson, and…it just came to me: What Anson had done to Spain, Frank was going to do to Heyoka—pirate the Nation's gold; the oil. That meant there had to be an oil well on Point Disappointment. All the work going on to make space for *Centurion* covered the work for a secret oil pump."

Ann's mother twirled a glass of champagne and her rings twinkled. "And not one, but two."

"One to pump oil out and the other to pump water in. That way the pressure in the field stays even, and the gauges in Heyoka don't show a drain. What I hear is the well is a very slow one in any case because it doesn't tap the mother oil directly, the oil just oozes from the main pool through a layer of porous rock into the bore hole on Point Disappointment.

"The Common Wealth geologists think the hole didn't start to fill until after it was capped. A few people in the gang that built the original terminal for old B.S. Bullard must have discovered it."

"The 'es. squad' of the journal?"

"Exactly," I said, "Es. probably stands for 'especial.' I bet the missing pages are explicit, but Mary says Frank Bullard burned them. If not for the killer flu after World War One…"

"Frank Bullard's grandfather would have been the pirate." Elizabeth Summerlune turned her gaze to the orange moon floating over the trees. "How ironic that Frank Bullard should plant the fatal clue by naming his ship *Centurion.* Do you think Frank knew the reference to Commodore Anson?

"Probably not. Anyway, I imagine the new ship was under construction and named by the time he discovered the journal entry and found the old well."

The bells in the clock tower rang the quarter-hour. At the seawall, I saw Arianna, Mary and Tom throw back their heads in laughter at a remark from Steve.

The best part of a month had passed since the collision and the sinking of *Taurus*. Police work had shown the crucial link in Connie's scheme was, as I guessed, Louise Harnet's relationship to the skipper of the PT boat.

When I saw the two of them and Connie and Althea Villeneuve at the Three Ohs Salooon, the Harnets thought I had figured out their check-counterfeiting scheme or would figure it out—that was why I was attacked. Connie was not part of it, though. It was just the Harnets.

Mark and John were going to toss me off the bluff at the cemetery. After a fall like that, no one would be able to sort out exactly how I had died.

Also, Mary told me, the Harnets thought Frank Bullard had killed his wife, but so far no one has cracked his alibi.

I idly sloshed the lime twist back and forth in my vodka and spotted Alice Emeu, dressed down and dowdy as usual in magenta sequins and yellow headband. Our eyes connected and she toddled over.

"You look like you've recovered from our adventure," I said, thinking, Migod, where does she get these outfits? The rest of us were clad in conservative gray or blue. She looked like the ubiquitous popinjay of poem and song.

"You bet, squirt. It's added years to my life and I'll take all of those I can get." She wheezed and I patted her spangled back.

"Shipmate, you're like your name."

"How so?"

"An emeu is a rare bird and so are you."

The webbing of her face shifted upward into a beam and we both laughed. She put her hand on my arm and stood on tiptoe to kiss my cheek.

"Aha," came the voice of Arianna from behind us, alone for thirty seconds and flirting away like mad." We turned to find her and Mary, grinning.

Alice placidly smoothed her yellow ribbons, said, "Oh, we're just two old shipmates having a gam. Gray suits you, Arianna. I love the off-white piping of the jacket, but what I really love is your emerald." The gem flashed green as she caught Arianna's hand and put it into mine. "He's all yours, my dear."

Turning to go, she said over her shoulder, "There's a piano over there under the awning. Later we'll sing. There are even a couple of songs that sound good with a marginal baritone, Hadrian. Meanwhile, eine kleine Mozart?"

"Of course," I said. She turned and looked at Arianna "A little Mendelssohn for you, missy?"

Arianna stuck out her tongue at Alice's retreating shimmer.

Steve came over and I asked, "What were you conspirators laughing about?"

Mary took Steve's arm, "Steve said you had 'put your foot in a nest of Harnets and been over-well-mm-ed.'"

It was silly, but Tom and I snorted and for some reason laughter captured us all. Maybe it was the relief of coming to the end of a very bad time together, or maybe it was the moon. Anyway, we howled. "Steve, that was genius."

I turned to Mary. "Speaking of genius, are you going to skip a grade and go directly to Detective?"

"Not unless I can definitely pin Ann's death on Bullard or Harnet. Harnet says Ann dove clear of the PT boat, unhurt. He figured she'd swum away underwater and was hiding behind a piling or between two of the boats in the marina. Harnet says he phoned Bullard and told him. Bullard says it never happened. He'd already left for Kennedy Airport."

"So, Harnet is saying Bullard killed her—maybe as she came out of the water—and then left." said Steve. "Was there time?"

"Ordinarily there might have been," said Mary. "But that night there was a major tie-up on the Interstate. It was closed for three hours. If he hadn't left when he said he did, he'd never have made it.

"Maybe he flew to Kennedy," said Arianna. "I think he has his own plane." She made a "V" with her hands. "It's got a tail like a butterfly."

"We checked that out already." Mary pulled a notebook from her purse and began flipping pages. "How do you happen to know about it?"

"I splurged one day and took a helicopter from the city. They were nice enough to drop me at the Arkady Island airfield. It's just an asphalt strip, you know. No tower or anything. Just a few hangars."

We all nodded. It was about two miles from the

marina, tiny, shabby, far too small for anything but private planes. "I saw him taxi and take off as I was walking away from the chopper. It's a lovely little plane. Robin's-egg blue with Navy striping. Like the one that flew over us that day at Flyaway."

Mary squinted at her notepad in the moonlight. "It's called a Beechcraft Baron. Apparently it's normally at the main Heyoka airport in Gusher. It was there that night and the whole time he was away." She snapped the book shut.

"Mary," I interrupted, "A Beech Baron is a twin. It has two engines and a typical, cruciform tail." I put a hand at right angles to my arm. "The only Beechcraft with a V-tail like Arianna described is a Bonanza. It has a single engine."

"You're sure of this?" She stared at the notebook as though it had bitten her.

I waved at the moon. "As sure as the moon will rise and set. There was an airport next to my Army post in Oklahoma. I took lessons. I've seen Bonanzas."

Mary yanked a cellular phone from her purse. "Look, this may be a real break. I've got to follow up—right now." She ran off, punching buttons. Steve went after her.

"Arianna, I think you've run out the plank for pirate Frank."

I hoped for a smile, however wan, but her eyes were

glistening. She whispered, "He actually did kill her, didn't he?" I gathered her up.

"Arianna, I..." Ah, shit, sure he did it. He conked her when she came home, dripping wet, loaded her in the car and slid her in at a dark corner of the air strip. Or he smacked her as she scrambled onto the embankment of the marina. To hell with him. My job was Arianna.

When Ann's mother came over a few minutes later, Arianna pulled herself together and we explained why Mary had run off.

"I think I'd better sit down," she said.

Arianna took one elbow and I the other and we walked her over to a table and eased her into one of the wicker chairs.

"Oh, God, and just when I thought I'd reconciled myself to never knowing." She turned away and covered her face with her hands.

I saw Tom coming from the direction of the piano and intercepted him.

"Alice is starting," he said." I told him what had happened and his face went flat. He looked toward Arianna and Ann's mother and said, "Guess we'd better call off the singing."

"No, Tom, I don't think we should do that. Someone give me a tissue and a moment. Arianna opened her purse and passed one to her, then came over and tugged my shirt. "Come on, let's sing."

"You go," I said. I need a minute, too." Arianna looked startled and in an instant had her purse open again.

Smiling, I pulled her to me and whispered, "No, no I'm all right. You and Tom go on. I'll only be a minute. Promise."

As I turned toward the water, Mrs. Summerlune got to her feet to join Tom and Arianna. As I passed the table I picked up the glass of champagne she left behind.

The music shifted from ornamental to nostalgic and they swung into an old song of seafaring farewell, the women's voices rising brightly over the dark rumble of Tom's bass. The tune wasn't exactly *Auld Lang Syne,* but it was an arrow from the same quiver,

May the winds be soft,
May the seas be at peace,
May nature smile and
Grant your every wish.

I WALKED TO the clock tower and paused, feeling the steady heartbeat of the timeless machine, listening to the song, watching the flicker and sway of moonlight and water, remembering Heyoka legend says the flashes in the waves under a moon are the spirits of drowned sailors.

I stood on the seawall and tilted wine into the darkness. "Fair winds, Shipmate," I whispered. "Fair winds and farewell."

I raised the last of the wine to the sky, drank it off and launched the glass high and away into the night.

The goblet hit the water spinning. It raised a splash—a tiny ghost who instantly vanished—and I turned away toward life, music and Arianna.

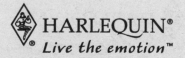